江汉大学研究生教材建设项目、江汉大学外国语学院教材资助项目

美国小说批评教程

刘晓燕　曾　莉　主编

http://press.hust.edu.cn
中国·武汉

内 容 提 要

本书共 22 章,每章包含两个部分:第一部分是小说家的背景介绍;第二部分是有关小说家或者小说作品的批评文章介绍。书中涉及关于 22 位美国著名小说家的批评文章,跨越整个美国文学史的多个历史时期。这些批评文章从不同的批评视角,运用不同的批评理论,采用不同的批评方法,对小说家及其作品的背景、文本、结构和主题等进行分析,具有一定的代表性。本教材重点在于美国小说批评文章的写作思路和批评方法,可供本科生和研究生学习使用。

图书在版编目(CIP)数据

美国小说批评教程/刘晓燕,曾莉主编. —武汉:华中科技大学出版社,2023.11
ISBN 978-7-5772-0173-3

Ⅰ.①美… Ⅱ.①刘… ②曾… Ⅲ.①小说评论-美国-教材 Ⅳ.①I712.074

中国国家版本馆 CIP 数据核字(2023)第 210920 号

美国小说批评教程   刘晓燕   曾 莉   主编

Meiguo Xiaoshuo Piping Jiaocheng

策划编辑:刘   平
责任编辑:江旭玉
封面设计:原色设计
责任监印:周治超

出版发行:华中科技大学出版社(中国·武汉)   电话:(027)81321913
            武汉市东湖新技术开发区华工科技园   邮编:430223

录   排:华中科技大学出版社美编室
印   刷:武汉开心印印刷有限公司
开   本:787mm×1092mm   1/16
印   张:12.75
字   数:243 千字
版   次:2023 年 11 月第 1 版第 1 次印刷
定   价:58.00 元

本书若有印装质量问题,请向出版社营销中心调换
全国免费服务热线:400-6679-118   竭诚为您服务
版权所有   侵权必究

Contents

Chapter 1   Washington Irving   /1

Chapter 2   James Fenimore Cooper   /7

Chapter 3   Nathaniel Hawthorne   /11

Chapter 4   Herman Melville   /23

Chapter 5   Edgar Allan Poe   /40

Chapter 6   William Dean Howells   /53

Chapter 7   Henry James   /61

Chapter 8   Mark Twain   /76

Chapter 9   Theodore Dreiser   /87

Chapter 10   Jack London   /97

Chapter 11   Sherwood Anderson   /105

Chapter 12   F. S. Fitzgerald   /109

Chapter 13   Ernest Hemingway   /119

Chapter 14   William Faulkner   /129

Chapter 15   Katherine Anne Porter   /141

Chapter 16   Richard Wright   /151

Chapter 17   Joseph Heller   /164

Chapter 18   John Barth   /167

Chapter 19	Thomas Pynchon	/171
Chapter 20	Donald Barthelme	/181
Chapter 21	Joyce Carol Oates	/184
Chapter 22	Saul Bellow	/190

Chapter 1

Washington Irving

Washington Irving (1783-1859)

Born in 1783, the year in which the American Revolution ended, Washington Irving, son of a prosperous New York hardware merchant, became the first author of the new country to be acclaimed in England. Although he never wrote a novel indeed, his chief achievement resides in perhaps a dozen sketches and short stories. He was acknowledged as the first man of letters in the United States. He lived until 1859, much admired by Poe and Hawthorne. His grapplings with the darker side of human nature were foreign to his own sanguine temperament. Yet Irving had managed to win admiration from Scott, Coleridge, and Byron. By the time he published *The Sketch Book of Geoffrey Crayon, Gent*, his best work had been done. In the succeeding forty years, he, like his contemporary William Cullen Bryant, became enshrined as a living figurehead of literary culture in America, though the conditions of American life rapidly outstripped his preparation of inclination to treat them in his writing.

Critical Perspectives

1. Feminism

Claudia Stokes, in "Bachelor Sketches: Invisible Women in Irving's Domestic Writings", examines Washington Irving's domestic writings of the 1820s, and argues that Irving devised the sketch as the literary genre of bachelorhood. In lavish and detailed sketches of numerous homes, Irving created a literary counterpart of the still life, but the effect of these sketches depended on the excision of women's domestic labor and the portrayal of the home in a state of static readiness, with all housework already completed. Irving's tales, however, often depict women's hidden domestic activities and show the invisible labors that underlie his sketches. These tales, however, portray women's housework as a source of terror, and they provide an implicit explanation for his sketches' omissions. The home in Irving's writings is an appealing aesthetic spectacle, but it poses grave danger to the unwitting bachelor, and Irving suggests that it is better to remain detached and unsettled than to risk the perils of heterosexual intimacy.[1]

Laura Plummer and Michael Nelson, in "'Girls Can Take Care of Themselves': Gender and Storytelling in Washington Irving's *The Legend of Sleepy Hollow*", examine the work of writer Washington Irving entitled "The Legend of Sleep Hollow". In Washington Irving's *The Legend of Sleepy Hollow*, notions of art are gender-based. The tale derives its tension from a conflict between male and female

---

[1] Stokes C. "Bachelor Sketches: Invisible Women in Irving's Domestic Writings". Early American Literature, 2022, 57(1): 193-219.

storytelling. The old wive's tales of the women serve to emasculate interlopers like Ichabod Crane through the the story of the headless horseman. The female-centered lore of the Dutch community defines the society and protects it from being altered by male notions of spirituality. This is a localized version of gendered storytelling, and would not seem realistic outside of its context. Topics discussed include presentation of the female gender, paradigm of masculine experience, storytelling and male imperialism, male storytelling and suppression of actual female speech, and presentation of female power in the story. ①

2. Cultural Study

C. Michael Hurst, in "Reinventing Patriarchy: Washington Irving and the Autoerotics of the American Imaginary", presents of the book *The Sketch Book of Geoffrey Crayon, Gent* by Washington Irving and edited by Susan Manning. Particular focus is given to the book's portrayal of patriarchy, including its relationship with English national identity and aristocracy. The author contends that the book's intent is to preserve American culture stability, through what is referred to as the autoerotic storytelling of its narrator Geoffrey Crayon. ②

3. New Historicism

Jerome McGann, in "Washington Irving, *A History of New York*, and American History", presents a literary criticism of the book *A History of New York* by

---

① Plummer L, Nelson M. "'Girls Can Take Care of Themselves': Gender and Storytelling in Washington Irving's *The Legend of Sleepy Hollow*". Studies in Short Fiction, 1993, 30(2): 175-184.

② Hurst C M. "Reinventing Patriarchy: Washington Irving and the Autoerotics of the American Imaginary". Early American Literature, 2012, 47(3):649-678.

Washington Irving. Particular focus is given to Irving's revisions to the text. Details on the roles of violence and intergroup conflict in the book are presented. Other topics include speculation, legend, and U.S. President Thomas Jefferson.①

Finn Pollard, in "From beyond the Grave and across the Ocean: Washington Irving and the Problem of Being a Questioning American, 1809-1820", reconsiders Washington Irving's early career between the productions of his first two major works: *A History of New York* (1809) and *The Sketch Book* (1819-1820). His life and writings in that period are treated as a study in the individual problem of being a "questioning American", specifically a questioning American writer, in the new republic, and as a broader critique of the developing new nation. Specifically, it places those writings in dialogue with the dominant Jeffersonian narrative of a glorious national future. It thus rediscovers Irving as a critical alternative witness to this important period in American history and the entwined attempt to critique his country and to come to terms with it as the central, underappreciated theme both in neglected writings (his contributions to *The Analectic Magazine*) and familiar tales (*Rip van Winkle*, and *The Legend of Sleepy Hollow*).②

Steven Petersheim, in "History and Place in the Nineteenth Century: Irving and Hawthorne in Westminster Abbey", argues that through their reflections on Westminster Abbey, Washington Irving and Nathaniel Hawthorne explore questions about the place of an American author on the world stage. Irving's positions the past as subservient to the present, probably as a result of America's newly re-established independence from the mother country after the War of 1812.

---

① McGann J. "Washington Irving, *A History of New York*, and American History". Early American Literature, 2012, 47(2): 349-376.

② Pollard F. "From beyond the Grave and across the Ocean: Washington Irving and the Problem of Being a Questioning American, 1809-1820". American Nineteenth Century History, 2007, 8(1): 81-101.

Hawthorne's sketches on English life, on the other hand, depict the past not as fading into oblivion but as immortal, a stance that perhaps reflects America's struggle for self-redefinition in the face of the national dissolution threatened by the approaching civil war. For Hawthorne, and in part for Irving as well, Old England is the seedbed of New England—a place in which an American can more fully comprehend his or her own place in the world. For both authors, the past as represented by Westminster Abbey is a productive and interactive site of literary appreciation, development, participation, and critique. [1]

Jeffrey Insko, in "Diedrich Knickerbocker, Regular Bred Historian", presents literary criticism of the book *A History of New York* by Washington Irving. It examines the role of historians in unearthing knowledge, as exemplified by his protagonist, Diedrich Knickerbocker. It explores the concepts of both epistemology, or the process by which historical knowledge is arrived at, and temporality, or the process by which historical is experienced. [2]

Sarah Richardson, in "Gotham Gift Giver", discusses the ways in which the 1837 painting *St. Nicholas*, by artist Robert Weir, reflect the stories of U.S. author Washington Irving and the Dutch origins of New York State. Focus is given to the symbolism of the painting, along with St. Nicholas' role as the patron saint of the Dutch colony of New Amsterdam. [3]

4. Biographical Study

Andrew Kopec, in "Irving, Ruin, and Risk", discusses author Washington

---

[1] Petersheim S. "History and Place in the Nineteenth Century: Irving and Hawthorne in Westminster Abbey". College Literature, 2012, 39(4): 118-137.

[2] Insko J. "Diedrich Knickerbocker, Regular Bred Historian". Early American Literature, 2008, 43(3): 605-641.

[3] Richardson S. "Gotham Gift Giver". American History, 2014, 48(6): 19.

Irving's decision to become a professional writer in the early 19th century. It is argued that Irving largely decided to write and publish his most famous work, *The Sketch Book*, due to the anxiety he felt over his brother, who failed the import-export firm, P. & E. Irving. The author is also more broadly concerned with the connection between identity and markets in the work.①

---

① Kopec A. "Irving, Ruin, and Risk". Early American Literature, 2013, 48(3): 709-735.

Chapter 2

James Fenimore Cooper

James Fenimore Cooper (1789-1851)

James Fenimore Cooper will always be remembered first for his *Leatherstocking Tales*: *The Pioneers*, *The Last of the Mohicans*, *The Prairie*, *The Pathfinder*, and *The Deerslayer*. These five books recount the experiences of an American frontiersman, variously named Deerslayer, Hawkeye, Pathfinder, Leatherstocking, and the Trapper, between the early 1740's, when British America was a line of settlements along the Atlantic coast, and 1805-1806, when the Lewis and Clark expedition crossed the continent. Though the books were not written in the order of the events they portray, they form, nonetheless, a kind of American epic, concerned not only with the opening of the West, but also with the costs involved in the process: the cutting of the forests, the killing of the game, and the displacement of the Indian. Leather Stocking, a man of the woods, wants to preserve the natural environment and use it only as needed, but by acting as hunter and scout, he opens the wilderness to the very setters whose wasteful ways he abhors.

Critical Perspectives

1. New Historicism

Marek Paryz, in "The Last of the Black Snakes and *The Last of the Mohicans*", explores the influence of James Fenimore Cooper on Polish writers who published books and stories featuring American Indians in the late nineteenth and early twentieth centuries. The first part of the article offers an analysis of two texts by Henryk Sienkiewicz. Sienkiewicz's readiness to develop his own ideas of American Indians is confirmed by his short story *Sachem*, in which he employs the Cooperman trope of the last surviving member of the tribe in a way that evidently transcends the limits of prejudiced representations. The second part of the article is devoted to the Polish adaptations of *The Leatherstocking Tales* by Maria Julia Zaleska and P. Laskowski, with a particular focus on the two authors' strategies of familiarizing the Polish reader with an alien subject matter. [1]

Bill Christophersen, in "*The Last of the Mohicans* and the Missouri Crisis", presents a literary criticism of the book *The Last of the Mohicans* by James Fenimore Cooper. According to the author, the book indirectly discusses issues surrounding slavery through its discussion of the history of Native American peoples in the U. S. It is suggested that the book deals specifically with the Missouri Crisis of 1819 and the 1822 Denmark Vesey Conspiracy. Topics discussed include slave insurrections, emancipation, and empathy. [2]

---

[1] Paryz M. "The Last of the Black Snakes and *The Last of the Mohicans*". European Journal of American Culture, 2012, 31(3): 219-230.

[2] Christophersen B. "*The Last of the Mohicans* and the Missouri Crisis". Early American Literature, 2011, 46(2): 263-289.

Simon Edwards, in "The Geography of Violence: Historical Fiction and the National Question", examines the representation and justification of acts of violence in historical novels from different national literatures. Topics discussed include background on descriptions of acts of capital punishment in historical novels; details in the works of James Fenimore Cooper; and analysis of the novel *The Fatal Environment*, by Richard Slotkin. [1]

Michael Schnell, in "The For(e)gone Conclusion: *The Leatherstocking Tales* as Antebellum History", discusses the criticisms upon images of the extinction of ethnic groups in *The Leatherstocking Tales*. Topics discusses include extinction as foregone conclusion in James Fenimore Cooper's historical narrative; ethnic conflict obliterating ethnic difference; ethnic conflict in a violent end; cultural and ethnic separateness; concept of antebellum typology; and cultural mixing and extinction. [2]

Peter Shawn Taylor, in "Losing *The Last of the Mohicans*", discusses the social significance of the book *The Last of the Mohicans*, by James Fenimore Cooper. Particular attention is given to Hawk-eye, the protagonist in the text, who is largely seen as the model for Hollywood's most famous creation, the cowboy. Other topics include the merit of Cooper's literary works, his place among American authors of the 19th century, as well as a historical review of the Canada/New York border during the time of the Native Americans. [3]

2. Thematic Study

Ian Dennis, in "Radical Father, Moderate Son: Cooper's Lionel Lincoln",

---

[1] Edwards S. "The Geography of Violence: Historical Fiction and the National Question". Novel: A Forum on Fiction, 2001, 34(2): 293-308.

[2] Schnell M. "The For(e)gone Conclusion: *The Leatherstocking Tales* as Antebellum History". American Transcendental Quarterly, 1996, 10(4): 331-348.

[3] Taylor P S. "Losing *The Last of the Mohicans*". Maclean's, 2007, 120(28): 63.

presents a critique of James Fenimore Cooper's novel *Lionel Lincoln*. It's about a young American-born officer and his relationship with his father. Topics discussed include Lionel Lincoln's return to his home in Boston, Massachusetts during the outbreak of the American Revolution; fictional flaws in Cooper's novel; and the strange, powerful father in *Lionel Lincoln*. ①

3. Gender Study

Yvette R. Piggush, in "Modernity, Gender, and the Panorama in Early Republican Literature", examines the ways in which panoramas, as they were discussed in early American Republican literature, were connected to early American gender relations and social mobility, particularly in the way that panoramas were meant to be viewed within the home by women. Focus is given to such literary works as *The Pioneers* by James Fenimore Cooper, and *A Trip to Niagara* by William Dunlap. ②

Sandra Tomc, in "'Clothes upon Sticks': James Fenimore Cooper and the Flat Frontier", presents literary criticism of the novel *The Deerslayer* by James Fenimore Cooper. It presents the characters and explores the symbolic significance of these characters. It examines the representation of whiteness, race discrimination and destiny in the novel. An overview of the story of the novel is also provided. ③

---

① Dennis I. "Radical Father, Moderate Son: Cooper's Lionel Lincoln". American Transcendental Quarterly, 1997, 11(2): 77-91.
② Piggush Y R. "Modernity, Gender, and the Panorama in Early Republican Literature". Early American Literature, 2013, 48(2): 425-456.
③ Tomc S. "'Clothes upon Sticks': James Fenimore Cooper and the Flat Frontier". Texas Studies in Literature and Language, 2009, 51(2): 142-178.

Chapter 3

Nathaniel Hawthorne

Nathaniel Hawthorne (1804-1864)

Nathaniel Hawthorne's fiction is unique in two important respects. He was the first major novelist in English to combine high moral seriousness with transcendent dedication to art. He was also the first major novelist in English that insist upon the basic unreality of his words. As an imaginative genius gifted with considerable linguistic skill, he opened a path in literature that few have followed with comparable success. Like all great writers, he was original in that fundamental sense in which the work resists duplication because it remains identified with the relative individuality of the author. George Eliot (1819-1880) followed Hawthorne in the attempt to wed morality to art, but she attempted the fusion with in a framework of realistic verisimilitude. Most writers since Hawthorne who have worked outside of the framework of realism have been less concerned than he with the moral seriousness of their works.

Critical Perspectives

1. New Historicism

Marty Roth, in "The World of the Fathers: Hawthorne in *The Custom-House*", argues that Nathaniel Hawthorne's essay *The Custom-House* takes the form of a classic nekuia, a descent into the underworld to confront the dead but commanding father and redeem a saving cultural message or vision. The custom-house is the setting for this journey, which takes the form of a series of spectral encounters. Hawthorne refuses to acknowledge the initial supplicants (King Derby, John and William Hathorne), but acquiesces to the demands of a third, Surveyor Pue. As is well-known, the essay has a problematic relationship with the romance that follows it. For one thing, Hawthorne of *The Custom-House* is a spent force, a failed romancer. In *The Scarlet Letter*, Hawthorne both defies his Puritan ancestors and accedes to their wishes. [1]

Thomas J. Balcerski, in "'A Work of Friendship': Nathaniel Hawthorne, Franklin Pierce, and the Politics of Enmity in the Civil War Era", investigates the friendship of Nathaniel Hawthorne and Franklin Pierce over the period 1852-1868. By revealing an intimate, later-life friendship between the two men, it underscores the role of enmity toward others in shaping the friendships of political actors in the Civil War era. It examines the development of this friendship through three different phases of their lives. First, the period of partisan activity in the presidential election

---

[1] Roth M. "The World of the Fathers: Hawthorne in *The Custom-House*". Canadian Review of American Studies, 2021, 51(2): 83-91.

of 1852, during which time Hawthorne wrote *The Life of Franklin Pierce* (1852); second, the period of separation and reunion abroad, including Hawthorne's controversial dedication to Pierce in *Our Old Home*: *A Series of English Sketches* (1863); and third, the author's final journey with Pierce, Hawthorne's subsequent death, and Pierce's embrace of members of Hawthorne's family in the ex-president's remaining years. This article argues that the friendship of Hawthorne and Pierce had been transformed by the divisive forces of partisanship, which in turn altered each man's view of his friendships with others. ①

Constance C. T. Hunt, in "The Persistence of Theocracy: Hawthorne's *The Scarlet Letter*", argues that Nathaniel Hawthorne's *The Scarlet Letter* can provide insight into the persistent appeal of the moral and political certitudes that theocracy offers and that can serve as a corrective to liberal secularism's often myopic tendency to downplay the continuing moral and political appeal of religious belief and authority. Focusing on three puzzles raised in the structure and narrative of *The Scarlet Letter*, the article explores Hawthorne's consideration of theocracy as a foundation in the past, as an antidote to the modern tendency toward materialism, and as a persistent alternative that deserves continued reflection. ②

Matthew S. Holland, in "Remembering John Winthrop—Hawthorne's Suggestion", argues that influential but obscure, admired and loathed, utterly rejected by some on the left even as other liberals vigorously battle conservatives to make him an icon of party ideals, John Winthrop, first governor of Massachusetts, is unique in our civic consciousness. Quite unexpectedly, Nathaniel Hawthorne— one of American Puritanism's earliest, fiercest, and most brilliant critics—gives us reason to recover a picture of Winthrop that acknowledges his more admirable virtues

---

① Balcerski T J. "'A Work of Friendship': Nathaniel Hawthorne, Franklin Pierce, and the Politics of Enmity in the Civil War Era". Journal of Social History, 2017, 50(4): 655-679.

② Hunt C C T. "The Persistence of Theocracy: Hawthorne's *The Scarlet Letter*". Perspectives on Political Science, 2009, 38(1): 25-32.

and contributions without sparing condemnation of the Puritan political regime he did so much to establish. [1]

2. Gender Study

Kelly Masterson, in "'As Nice a Little Saleswoman, as I Am a Housewife': Domesticity, Education, and Separate Spheres in Nathaniel Hawthorne's *The House of the Seven Gables*", considers Nathaniel Hawthorne's intervention into the separate spheres ideology in *The House of the Seven Gables*. By depicting Phoebe Pyncheon's domestic and industrial skills, Hawthorne raises the possibility of women successfully negotiating the business world but contains them within the home by merging marketplace values and domestic education principles. [2]

3. Narratology

Julia Fisher, in "Hawthorne's Allegory", focuses on the American novelist Nathaniel Hawthorne, who operated in a world where allegory was more or less taboo. He went out of his way to label himself a "romancer" rather than an allegorist and was at times as quick as anyone to condemn allegory. Yet he also wrote a number of tales that are, in various ways, undeniably allegorical. Critics have studied Hawthorne's allegories as they support other elements of his fiction: his formal positioning of his own writing, his particular take on romance, his political and theological views, and much more. The author of this essay proposes

---

[1] Holland M S. "Remembering John Winthrop—Hawthorne's Suggestion". Perspectives on Political Science, 2007, 36(1): 4-14.

[2] Masterson K. "'As Nice a Little Saleswoman, as I Am a Housewife': Domesticity, Education, and Separate Spheres in Nathaniel Hawthorne's *The House of the Seven Gables*". Canadian Review of American Studies, 2018, 48(2): 191-209.

that Hawthorne's allegories are self-conscious—they interrogate the nature, purpose, and value of allegory. It mentions that allegory is a way of thinking, and suggests a certain epistemology; it also mentions that he found himself at the convergence of two traditions from America, an allegorically steeped religious tradition, and from the English romantics, a self-proclaimed anti-allegorical tradition. ①

Uğur Uçum, in "A Reconsideration of Nathaniel Hawthorne's *The Scarlet Letter*", aims at offering an in-depth analysis of the 1926 and the 1995 movie adaptations of Nathaniel Hawthorne's 1850 novel *The Scarlet Letter*. Caught in a story of love and shame, of sin and salvation, Hester Prynne oscillates between Roger Chillingworth and Arthur Dimmesdale, two men too coward to bear the consequences of their actions. Why is Hester's story still fascinating today? Will contemporary readers be willing to read the 1850 novel? Which are the main differences between the two movie adaptations? These are only a few of the questions this paper focuses upon. ②

Lydia G. Fash, in "The Chronicle and the Reckoning: A Temporal Paradox in Hawthorne's *Twice-Told Tales*", talks about the short story collection *Twice-Told Tales* by Nathaniel Hawthorne, focusing on the book's temporality and readers' attitudes regarding their foreknowledge of plot developments. ③

Sean J. Kelly, in "Hawthorne's 'Material Ghosts': Photographic Realism and Liminal Selfhood in *The House of the Seven Gables*", presents a literary criticism of the 1851 novel *The House of the Seven Gables* by Nathaniel Hawthorne. The author discusses artistic metaphor in Hawthorne's novel and how Hawthorne's reaction to photographic realism in 19th-century daguerreotype photography influences the theme

---

① Fisher J. "Hawthorne's Allegory". Raritan, 2020, 39(4): 112-124.
② Uçum U. "A Reconsideration of Nathaniel Hawthorne's *The Scarlet Letter*". Journal of History, Culture & Art Research, 2015, 4(3): 118-126.
③ Fash L G. "The Chronicle and the Reckoning: A Temporal Paradox in Hawthorne's *Twice-Told Tales*". Narrative, 2013, 21(2): 221-242.

of self in the novel. Also discussed is Hawthorne's reaction to pre-Raphaelite painters and Dutch masters at the 1857 Manchester Arts Exhibition in England.①

Edward Wesp, in "Beyond the Romance: The Aesthetics of Hawthorne's *Chiefly about War Matters*", discusses Nathaniel Hawthorne's position on slavery and the course of the post-Civil War U. S. in his 1862 essay for journal *The Atlantic Monthly*, *Chiefly about War Matters*. It cites a passage from the essay whose aesthetic quality is seen as an emblem of his indifference to slavery and the power of celebratory versions of American Renaissance literature. It indicates how its political and artistic crises revealed his literary art as an experimental literature that clarifies the means by which aesthetics find expression and why art matters.②

Michèle Bonnet, in "Consuming Tragedy and 'the Little Cannibal' in *The House of the Seven Gables*", explores the depiction of tragedy in the 1851 novel *The House of the Seven Gables*, by Nathaniel Hawthorne. The characters in the novel are described in detail. It explains the reasons why the composition of the romance was such a lengthy and laborious process. It explores the recurrent episodes revolving around Ned Higgins. The article describes how the tale dramatizes a series of encounters between a child and creatures whose destructive power is signified. The ways to expose the illusory character of the tragic vision are outlined.③

Magnus Ullén, in "Reading with 'the Eye of Faith': The Structural Principle of Hawthorne's Romances", discusses the principle of chiastic inversion in romance fiction written by Nathaniel Hawthorne, which is designed to make readers an integral part of the romance by challenging their capacity for faith. Topics

---

① Kelly S J. "Hawthorne's 'Material Ghosts': Photographic Realism and Liminal Selfhood in *The House of the Seven Gables*". Papers on Language and Literature, 2011, 47(3): 227-260.

② Wesp E. "Beyond the Romance: The Aesthetics of Hawthorne's *Chiefly about War Matters*". Texas Studies in Literature and Language, 2010, 52(4): 408-432.

③ Bonnet M. "Consuming Tragedy and 'the Little Cannibal' in *The House of the Seven Gables*". American Transcendental Quarterly, 2006, 20(2): 481-497.

discussed include overview of the chiastic pattern in the novel *The Scarlet Letter*; structural division of the twenty-one chapters of the romance *The House of the Seven Gables*; and reflection of the complex interplay among money, sexuality and death in the novel *The Blithedale Romance*. ①

Cindy Lou Daniels, in "Hawthorne's Pearl: Woman-Child of the Future", presents literary criticisms on the book *The Scarlet Letter*, by Nathaniel Hawthorne. The beauty of Hawthorne's defining work is that it lends itself to contemporary analysis year after year, decade after decade. As each change in society asserts itself, critics look at Hawthorne's *The Scarlet Letter* with a fresh perspective and find the story ripe with new meaning that is relevant to contemporary society. Ending the novel, Hawthorne writes of the mystery of his character Pearl in terms of the future. If still alive, she must now have been in the flush and bloom of early womanhood, and there were some who faithfully believed Pearl was not only alive, but married and happy, and mindful of her mother, and that she would most joyfully have entertained that sad and lonely mother at her fireside. ②

David V. Urban, in "Evasion of the Finite in Hawthorne's *The Artist of the Beautiful*", focuses on the concept of what is finite as seen in the character of Owen Warland in Nathaniel Hawthorne's *The Artist of the Beautiful*. Warland's sacrifice of human love and the strength of earthly reality in his quest for artistic perfection, as well as Owen's recognition of his need for the finite in his progression as an artist and as a man, is addressed. ③

---

① Ullén M. "Reading with 'the Eye of Faith': The Structural Principle of Hawthorne's Romances". Texas Studies in Literature and Language, 2006, 48(1): 1-36.

② Daniels C L. "Hawthorne's Pearl: Woman-Child of the Future". American Transcendental Quarterly, 2005, 19(3): 221-236.

③ Urban D V. "Evasion of the Finite in Hawthorne's *The Artist of the Beautiful*". Christianity & Literature, 2005, 54(3): 343-358.

4. Psychological Analysis

Eric Savoy, in "Nathaniel Hawthorne and the Anxieties of the Archive", presents that Robert K. Martin published an important essay that explored the gendered anxiety of authorship that left its traces throughout Nathaniel Hawthorne's career. Given that novel-writing was understood in mid-nineteenth-century America as an essentially feminine occupation, did Hawthorne perceive himself as emasculated? Savoy supplements Martin's argument by taking up the "fiction" of authorship, specifically the personage of Nathaniel Hawthorne that is constructed in *The Custom-House*. Previously, Savoy focused on Hawthorne's gothic poetics as the figurative matrix within which the "author" accepts the exhortation of Surveyor Pue to fulfill his "filial duty" by delivering to the public the historical romance of Hester Prynne. This article explores the "psychic economy" of what Jacques Derrida conceptualizes as the event of the archive—that is, the performative ways in which subjects are constituted precisely as subjects, in conformity with the regulatory ideals of nation, religious tradition, and gender. If there is no subject without a subtending and largely mythical archive of cultural practice, then *The Custom-House* is a spectacular mise-en-scène—rhetorically rich and charged with affect—of the ritualistic protocols of assujettissement. [①]

Martin Bidney, in "Fire, Flutter, Fall, and Scatter: A Structure in the Epiphanies of Hawthorne's Tales", shows that there is an epiphanic moment at certain points in the stories of novelist Nathaniel Hawthorne, in which moral categories disperse into four image—motifs namely fire, flutter, fall and scatter. The psychoanalytic implications in the epiphanic formula in Hawthorne are

---

① Savoy E. "Nathaniel Hawthorne and the Anxieties of the Archive". Canadian Review of American Studies, 2015, 45(1): 38-66.

discussed. It is concluded by the author that, with the central vision of the short story *Young Goodman Brown*, an exhibit whose enigmatic fascination can be contextualized when it is seen as a Hawthornean epiphany with no explicit indication of a fall.①

5. Social Study

Huang Zhongfeng, in "From 'Purified with Fire' to 'that Impression of Permanence': Holgrave's Conversion in *The House of the Seven Gables*", presents literary criticism on the book *The House of the Seven Gables* by Nathaniel Hawthorne. It outlines the characters and explores their symbolic significance. Topics include investigation of the three phases of Holgrave's character of the book, perspective of social reform, and examination of the inseparable relationship between Hawthorne's reformist impulse and historical consciousness. Also an overview of the story is given.②

Dustin Hannum, in "Sermons out of Rags: Constitutionalism, Conspiracy Theory, and Reading *The Scarlet Letter* in Hawthorne's Custom-House", presents literary criticism of the book *The Scarlet Letter* by Nathaniel Hawthorne. Particular focus is given to the roles of aesthetics and politics in the novel's introductory sketch titled "The Custom-House". According to the author, the sketch illustrates tensions over the interpretation of the U. S. Constitution and its significance for the future of slavery in America. Topics discussed include literary theorist Delia Bacon

---

① Bidney M. "Fire, Flutter, Fall, and Scatter: A Structure in the Epiphanies of Hawthorne's Tales". Texas Studies in Literature and Language, 2008, 50(1): 58-89.

② Huang Zhongfeng. "From 'Purified with Fire' to 'that Impression of Permanence': Holgrave's Conversion in *The House of the Seven Gables*". Papers on Language and Literature, 2019, 55(2): 144-167.

and the religious concept of Providence.①

Christopher Leise, in "The Eye-ball and the Butterfly: Beauty and the Individual Soul in Emerson and Hawthorne", discusses the concept of selfhood by authors Ralph Waldo Emerson and Nathaniel Hawthorne. Topics discussed include Emerson and Hawthorne's competing definitions of beauty, the distinctions between Emerson's and Hawthorne's idea of a self's fullest realization, and the parallels between the two thinkers' notion of beauty and virtues.②

6. Thematic Study

Edward A. Abramson, in "Gardens and Edens: Nathaniel Hawthorne's *Rappaccini's Daughter* and Bernard Malamud's *The Lady of the Lake*", explores the parameters of the link between gardens and Edens in the two stories, *Rappaccini's Daughter*, by Nathaniel Hawthorne, and *The Lady of the Lake*, by Bernard Malamud, to illustrate their concern with the complexities of morality based on biblical and mythological contexts. It analyzes the themes of Adam and Eve motifs, Jewish identity and the Holocaust. It also examines implications of the garden for the heroes' perceptions of the heroines.③

Richard E. Meyer, in "'Death Possesses a Good Deal of Real Estate': References to Gravestones and Burial Grounds in Nathaniel Hawthorne's *American Notebooks* and *Selected Fictional Works*", examines Nathaniel Hawthorne's use of

---

① Hannum D. "Sermons out of Rags: Constitutionalism, Conspiracy Theory, and Reading *The Scarlet Letter* in Hawthorne's Custom-House". Papers on Language and Literature, 2015, 51(2): 140-169.

② Leise C. "The Eye-ball and the Butterfly: Beauty and the Individual Soul in Emerson and Hawthorne". Philological Quarterly, 2013, 92(4): 471-497.

③ Abramson E A. "Gardens and Edens: Nathaniel Hawthorne's *Rappaccini's Daughter* and Bernard Malamud's *The Lady of the Lake*". Studies in Short Fiction, 2012, 37(1): 27-42.

graveyards as settings and plot elements in his book *American Notebooks*. Most of Hawthorne's interesting uses of burial grounds and gravestones in his fiction are directly related to specific entries he made in *American Notebooks*. Literal graveyards such as the Charter Street Burial Ground in Salem, Massachusetts, and Kings' Chapel Burial Ground in Boston, Massachusetts, inspired Hawthorne's use of graveyards in fiction. In the course of his lifetime, Hawthorne experience first hand the transformation from village graveyard to rural cemetery as the dominant funerary landscape in the U. S. ①

7. Cultural Study

Olivia Gatti Taylor, in "Cultural Confessions: Penance and Penitence in Nathaniel Hawthorne's *The Scarlet Letter* and *The Marble Faun*", offers a literary criticism of the novels *The Scarlet Letter* and *The Marble Faun*, both by Nathaniel Hawthorne, in which the author explores themes of penance and penitence. The author provides an analysis of sin, guilt, and redemption in the works and explores their impact on individuality in the community settings of the novels, that is, in Puritan New England and in urban Rome, Italy. ②

Lee Trepanier, in "The Need for Renewal: Nathaniel Hawthorne's Conservatism", details the efforts of conservative thinker Nathaniel Hawthorne to renew the Puritan tradition through the power of art. Topics discussed include criticism of writer Russell Kirk's portrayal of Hawthorne in his book *The Conservative*

---

① Meyer R E. "'Death Possesses a Good Deal of Real Estate': References to Gravestones and Burial Grounds in Nathaniel Hawthorne's *American Notebooks* and *Selected Fictional Works*". Studies in the Literary Imagination, 2006, 39(1): 1-28.

② Taylor O G. "Cultural Confessions: Penance and Penitence in Nathaniel Hawthorne's *The Scarlet Letter* and *The Marble Faun*". Renascence, 2005, 58(2): 134-152.

Mind; analysis of Hawthorne's doctrine of forgiveness; and reasons behind Hawthorne's political indifference. ①

8. Feminism

Angela M. Kelsey, in "Mrs. Wakefield's Gaze: Femininity and Dominance in Nathaniel Hawthorne's *Wakefield*", examines Nathaniel Hawthorne's short story entitled "Wakefield" through a feminist perspective. Topics discussed include the use of Michel Foucault's arguments in his book *The History of Sexuality*, *Volume 1*; analysis of the characters Mr. and Mrs. Wakefield; and analysis of the role of the narrator in the story. ②

Monika Elbert, in "The Surveillance of Woman's Body in Hawthorne's Short Stories", presents a surveillance of a woman's body in Nathaniel Hawthorne's works. In many of his female-centered stories, Hawthorne shows the need to control woman's sexuality or to insist upon her purity with a type of morality play whose sexual dynamics correspond to the theories of 19th century sexuality. There was a strange obsession and manifestation with sexuality, which was expressed in the many advice books and control mechanisms, but which ultimately had an outlet in the many varied forms of the discourse of sexuality, of which woman was often the central protagonist. ③

---

① Trepanier L. "The Need for Renewal: Nathaniel Hawthorne's Conservatism". Modern Age, 2003, 45(4): 315-323.
② Kelsey A M. "Mrs. Wakefield's Gaze: Femininity and Dominance in Nathaniel Hawthorne's *Wakefield*". American Transcendental Quarterly, 1994, 8(1): 17-31.
③ Elbert M. "The Surveillance of Woman's Body in Hawthorne's Short Stories". Women's Studies, 2004, 33(1): 23-46.

Chapter 4
Herman Melville

Herman Melville (1819-1891)

What characterizes Herman Melville's novels from *Typee* trough *Moby-Dick* is the sense of an immanent personality, the author through his narrator, examining himself, his experiences, and the world about him. This personality seeks categorical answers and finds none, and, when his quest fails, seeks ways to survive in an inscrutable universe. In these novels, the theme of the autobiographical quest signaled the presence of a first-person narrator and the less identification of settings and events with the facts of Melville's life as a sailor. If the writings after *Moby-Dick* seem less autobiographical, its is because Melville places more distance between himself and his stories. His protagonists are more obviously interior and spiritual voyagers to less romantic places, and an omniscient author, skeptical though compassionate, has displaced the roving, questing youth who spins high-spirited tales of his travels.

Critical Perspectives

1. Thematic Study

Yoshiaki Furui, in "Transnational Intimacy in *Israel Potter*", reads Herman Melville's *Israel Potter* by attending to the eponymous character's feeling of loneliness as an exile, which compels an examination of the relationship between individual and community. Building on Jean-Luc Nancy's concept of "inoperative community", which emerges between the dead and the living, the author of this essay argues that the community proposed in *Israel Potter* is informed by the belatedness that escapes containment by a political institution. [①]

Gregg Crane, in "The Hard Case: *Billy Budd* and the Judgment Intuitive", explores the importance of a certain form of intuitive reasoning to hard cases, ambiguous situations, and problems that seem to resist the straightforward application of a clear rule. Certain aspects of the processes of judgment come into sharpest relief in those cases where justice seems to require that we bend, modify, or repress the applicable rules. Judges have often been judged not only by virtue of their adherence to the procedures and norms of law, but also in regard to their ability to qualify or moderate or even subvert such rules. Melville's posthumous novel, *Billy Budd*, offers a revealing and even iconic instance of the necessity of

---

① Furui Y. "Transnational Intimacy in *Israel Potter*". Texas Studies in Literature and Language, 2022, 64(2): 1-20.

intuitive reasoning to these more arduous and uncertain forms of judgment. ①

Todd Goddard, in "'Thy Placeless Power': Melville, Mobility, and the Poetics of Placelessness", investigates Melville's unease with the erosion and absence of abiding places, which in turn are linked to proliferating spatial mobilities in the first half of the nineteenth century. "Although critics have pointed to Melville's celebration of travel and its attendant freedom of movement, few have commented on his concern for the consequences of mobility on the integrity of place or the resultant implications of placelessness for identity and authorship alike. What we see in Melville's works, I argue, and particularly in *Moby-Dick*, is a place-anxiety or place-panic that derives in part from the accelerating velocities of modernity and a sense of the increasing loss of stable, bordered, and bounded places. Melville's is thus an early voice antedating current cultural debates and ecocritical concerns over the role of place, the synergies and antagonisms between the local and the global, and the tensions between the rooted and the mobile. Melville's novels describe the consequences of the velocities of modern life and envision how its ever-increasing matrix of non-places may be navigated."②

2. Ecological Studies

Chantelle Bayes, in "Let the Animals Speak: Postromantic Renegotiations of the Animal Voice in *Only the Animals*", argues that writers of the Romantic tradition have often sought a reconciliation with nature, and animals have provided a source of connection through which writers can explore the human-nonhuman relationship.

---

① Crane G. "The Hard Case: *Billy Budd* and the Judgment Intuitive". University of Toronto Quarterly, 2013, 82(4): 889-906.
② Goddard T. "'Thy Placeless Power': Melville, Mobility, and the Poetics of Placelessness". Journal of the Utah Academy of Sciences, Arts & Letters, 2016(93): 247-258.

Animal welfare, animal rights and vegetarianism were some of the considerations advanced by Romantic writers of the time questioning Cartesian ideas of animals as mechanistic. Mary Shelley and Herman Melville used anthropomorphic creatures to explore the human-nonhuman animal boundary and advance the idea of nonhuman animals as conscious and agential beings. The author of this essay examines *Only the Animals* by Ceridwen Dovey, a contemporary novel which seeks to reconsider the animal voice in post-Romantic literary fiction. The author also considers the influence of posthumanist thinking on representation and the relationships between human and nonhuman animals with reference to the work of Marc Bekoff and Cary Wolfe. [1]

3. New-historicism

Muna Abd-Rabbo, in "The Naturalization of Orientalism in Herman Melville's *Mardi*: Whitewashing *Arabian Nights*?", refers that the nineteenth-century American novelist, Herman Melville, is oftentimes viewed as a multi-cultured innovator who possibly anticipated post-modernism. In his epic romance, *Mardi*, Melville incorporates aspects of Orientalism within a Westernized framework, thereby eroding cultural borders. This article focuses on *Arabian Nights* as one possible parent text for *Mardi* on the one hand, and on Melville's naturalization of certain Orientalist concepts in his novel on the other. Furthermore, it explores the question of whether Melville "whitewashes" the Eastern narrative to naturalize the text and thus familiarize Westerners with a foreign culture in the spirit of multi-culturalism, or whether he simply subscribes to the Orientalist stereotypes

---

[1] Bayes C. "Let the Animals Speak: Postromantic Renegotiations of the Animal Voice in *Only the Animals*". Social Alternatives, 2022, 41(3): 48-55.

prevalent in nineteenth-century America. ①

William Logan, in "Two Stray Notes on *Moby-Dick*", discusses the history of the publication of Herman Melville's 1851 novel *Moby-Dick*. Topics explored include the separate British and American copyrights obtained for the novel, the contract negotiation between Melville and American publisher Harper & Brothers, and the reviews earned by the novel published in various journals such as *The Spectator*, *Atlas*, and *The Morning Chronicle*. ②

Greg Grandin, in "Slavery & Freedom: Reading Melville in Post-9/11 America", offers opinions on the history of race relations in the U.S. and the history of attitudes towards Islam in Western countries. The true story on which book *Benito Cereno*, by Herman Melville, is discussed as an example of a lack of knowledge of the role of Islam in many of the Africans who became U.S. slaves. Melville is seen as an example of a tradition within the West in which Islam is both admired and feared as an opponent to the concept of extreme individualism. ③

Christopher Looby, in "Of Billy's Time: Temporality in Melville's *Billy Budd*", argues that *Billy Budd* is replete with invocations of various temporalities. This article brings the tale's "juggling temporalities" to bear upon the questions of sexuality, and the story also addresses and shows that *Billy Budd* is a searching exploration of (and meditation on) the profound historicity of sexuality. Unfinished and unpublished at the time of Melville's death, the extant manuscript of *Billy Budd* is a complicated palimpsest of additions and revisions. Reconstructing the genealogy of the manuscript's development reveals that Melville moved the action back in time. But there are several homosexuals in the text, who, although they

---

① Abd-Rabbo M. "The Naturalization of Orientalism in Herman Melville's *Mardi*: Whitewashing *Arabian Nights*?". Arab Studies Quarterly, 2020, 42(4): 273-286.

② Logan W. "Two Stray Notes on *Moby-Dick*". The New Criterion, 2021, 40(2): 13-18.

③ Grandin G. "Slavery & Freedom: Reading Melville in Post-9/11 America". The Nation, 2014, 298(4): 12-17.

ostensibly co-exist in one time and place, nevertheless belong to different historical regimes of sexuality. ①

Laura Barrett, in "'Light and Baffling': Uncanny Punning in Melville's *Benito Cereno*", presents a literary criticism of the novella *Benito Cereno* by Herman Melville. The author describes themes of the uncanny in the novella and discusses psychoanalyst Sigmund Freud's theory about the uncanny and death in relation to the novella. The author analyzes the uncanny in the language of the novella with particular focus on the character Amasa Delano. ②

4. Thematic Study

Ismail Khalaf Salih, Danear Jabbar AbdulKareem, and Omar Najem Abdullah, in "Monomaniac Revenge in Melville's *Moby Dick* and Bronte's *Wuthering Heights*", argue that revenge can be one of consequences of bad feeling towards others. This feeling of anger, hatred and prejudice could be based on traumatic visible or invisible experience. The level of that anger and hatred depends on the volume of damage caused by the action or judgment and, on other hand, it depends on man's endurance and tolerance upon that action or judgment. Revenge can be individual or collective as well. Individually, it is driven personally as a reaction of other's perceived harm when the individual desire is set to retaliate for bringing justice and satisfying his need. Collectively, most of ancient wars and conflicts were based on the concept of revenge which mostly brought collective devastation. This study utilizes rereading of the canonical texts, *Moby Dick* by Herman Melville and

---

① Looby C. "Of Billy's Time: Temporality in Melville's *Billy Budd*". Canadian Review of American Studies, 2015, 45(1): 23-37.

② Barrett L. "'Light and Baffling': Uncanny Punning in Melville's *Benito Cereno*". Papers on Language and Literature, 2011, 47(4): 404-429.

Wuthering Heights by Emily Bronte, to make better understanding of the "monomaniac revenge" by highlighting and analyzing the main characters in the two novels above, Ahab and Heathcliff, respectively, and their destructive revenge under the light of Psychological theory. Ahab was isolated from his family. Heathcliff was dismissed by his family. Later on they both lost their lives. Melville and Bronte prove that destructive revenge brings destructive results. The top focus of the study is on how Ahab and Heathcliff's excessive desire of revenge develops and then brings them and people around to death. [①]

Paul R. Cappucci, in "Down from the Crow's Nest: Herman Melville's *Battle-Pieces and Aspects of the War*", presents a critique of author Herman Melville's war-themed poetry collections *Battle-Pieces, and Aspects of the War*. It places Melville's work in the appropriate literary context and looks at Melville's emotional involvement in the American Civil War as seen in his poetry. It also examines two key manifestations of Melville's own depiction of the realities of the era. [②]

5. Psychoanalytical Study

J. Daniel Batt, in "Do This in Remembrance of Me: Bits and Pieces in Re-Membering the Body", presents a literary criticism of the novels *Moby-Dick*, by Herman Melville, and *Beloved*, by Toni Morrison. It examines the tension between the material and the spiritual explored in the books, the works' Biblical allusions and narratological structure, the division of the testaments at the moment of

---

① Salih I K, AbdulKareem D J, Abdullah O N. "Monomaniac Revenge in Melville's *Moby Dick* and Bronte's *Wuthering Heights*". e-Banji Journal, 2021, 18 (10): 107-116.

② Cappucci P R. "Down from the Crow's Nest: Herman Melville's *Battle-Pieces and Aspects of the War*". War, Literature and the Arts: An International Journal of the Humanities, 2005, 17(1/2): 162-169.

incarnation from a Christian perspective, the manifestation of the divine in the books, and the destruction of the body and death in the final stages of the archetypal incarnation.①

Andrew Schaap, in "Do You not See the Reason for Yourself? Political Withdrawal and the Experience of Epistemic Friction", argues that the epistemic friction that is generated when privileged subjects are confronted by different social perspectives is important for democratic politics since it can interrupt their active ignorance about oppressive social relations from which they benefit. However, members of oppressed groups might sometimes prefer not to accept the burden of educating the dominant. In circumstances of structural inequality, withdrawing from privileged subjects' ignorance can be a form of self-preservation. But such withdrawal also has the potential to induce epistemic friction insofar as it depletes the opportunities for active ignorance to reproduce itself. Herman Melville's tragicomic short story of Bartleby—the legal copyist who "would prefer not to" — has been celebrated by philosophers as emblematic of such resistant withdrawal. Interpreting the story as a dramatisation of the epistemic friction encountered by its narrator makes vivid how such withdrawal can be political.②

Yoshiaki Furui, in "Lonely Individualism in *Moby-Dick*", reconsiders the concept of individualism in Herman Melville's *Moby-Dick* by focusing on the affective aspect of Captain Ahab's solitude. By considering the cultural fervor over connectivity in antebellum America, due to what is known as the communications revolution, the author of this essay highlights Ahab's solitude, which stems from his misguided faith in his networked status with the white whale. Ahab's solitude has been understood as a manifestation of liberal individualism, which characterizes the

---

① Batt J D. "Do This in Remembrance of Me: Bits and Pieces in Re-Membering the Body". Renascence, 2021, 73(3): 161-170.

② Schaap A. "Do You not See the Reason for Yourself? Political Withdrawal and the Experience of Epistemic Friction". Political Studies, 2020, 68(3): 565-581.

ethos of mid-nineteenth-century America. However, what Ahab represents could be more accurately grasped by "lonely individualism". With its oxymoronic overtones, "lonely individualism" is intended to encapsulate the two valences of being alone: solitude and loneliness. By taking *Moby-Dick* as a case study, this essay seeks to join the critical endeavor of challenging the myth of individualism in Americanist literary studies by shedding light on the affective realm of an individualist. [1]

6. Gender Study

Robert K. Martin and Leland S. Person, in "'But Suppose I Did Want a Boy?': Homosexual Economies in Herman Melville's *The Confidence-Man*", center on chapter twenty-two of *The Confidence-Man*, the chapter in which the con man, in the guise of Philosophical Intelligence Officer, tries to sell a boy to Pitch, the misanthropic Missouri bachelor who has used up some thirty boys on his backwoods farm and now wants to replace boys with machines. Structured as an epistolary dialogue between the two authors, the article explores the complex ways in which Melville's novel positions its readers and the desires they bring to the text. Can the long debate in chapter twenty-two about buying boys be read as a transaction between a pimp and a pederast? Do other homosocial encounters in the novel encode homosexuality and thus reinforce our perception of it in chapter twenty-two? The authors argue for a queer reading of *The Confidence-Man* and in the process foreground their own sexual identities and reading practices. [2]

Richard Hardack, in "'Thou Shalt not Be Cozened': Incest, Self-Reliance, and the Portioning of Gendered Bodies in the Works of Herman Melville", examines

---

[1] Furui Y. "Lonely Individualism in *Moby-Dick*". Criticism, 2020, 62(4): 599.

[2] Martin R K, Person L S. "'But Suppose I Did Want a Boy?': Homosexual Economies in Herman Melville's *The Confidence-Man*". Canadian Review of American Studies, 2015, 45(1): 101-124.

actual and fantasized acts of incest in the literary works of author Herman Melville, including *Pierre*, *Mardi* and *Moby-Dick*. In several works, male characters imagine that incest might reunify them with a version of the concept of the term "all", or a collective form of identity. In order to address the extremes of male identity, Melville uses transcendental pantheism. It is suggested that incest in Melville's works becomes a proxy for redefining family and intimacy.①

7. Narratological Study

Sarah Thwaites, in "'Mirror with a Memory': Theories of Light and Preternatural Negatives in Herman Melville's *Moby-Dick*", explores theories of light in the American Romantic period as a way of addressing image-text relations in the dynamic early decades of photography. It addresses the gothic nature of the daguerreotype's ambiguous negative/positive picture and its temporal and spatial implications in relation to Melville's aesthetic of light in his Romantic epic *Moby-Dick*. Upon the daguerreotype's arrival in 1839, it was greeted by Americans with both fascination and suspicion: not only were the chemical exchanges viewed as wizardry and the picture deemed to take possession of the sitter's spirit, but when tilted under light, the daguerreotype's ghostly negative image is revealed. For Romantic artists, Daguerre's process, "the art of writing with light", held equally complex implications for the conception of nature. Newton's theory of light had already exposed its intricate character, but Goethe's nineteenth-century Colour Theory, with its descriptions of the individual nature of seeing, showed that the Romantic notion of nature as "light Divine" was deeply problematic. In *Moby-Dick*,

---

① Hardack R. "'Thou Shalt not Be Cozened': Incest, Self-Reliance, and the Portioning of Gendered Bodies in the Works of Herman Melville". Texas Studies in Literature and Language, 2013, 55 (3): 253-306.

Ishmael conflates meanings of whiteness, colour and light for more congruous poetic interpretations that mirror the daguerreotype's uncanny paradigm of light. ①

James Duban, in "Narrative Self-Absolution and Political Tyranny in *Moby-Dick* and *Darkness at Noon*", compares the characters of the book *Moby-Dick*, by Herman Melville, with the character of Nicolas Salmanovitch Rubashov in the novel *Darkness at Noon*, by Arthur Koestler, a reformed Communist Party member and Hungarian-British novelist. Koestler is said to have a rehabilitative identification with *Moby-Dick* and its character Ishmael. The political concerns and narrative artistry of *Moby-Dick* seem to reflect in Koestler's dramatization of totalitarianism. ②

Aaron McClendon, in "'For not in Words Can It Be Spoken': John Sullivan Dwight's Transcendental Music Theory and Herman Melville's *Pierre; or, The Ambiguities*", examines John Sullivan Dwight's transcendental music theories and how author Herman Melville's turn to music in his 1852 novel *Pierre; or, The Ambiguities*. In *Pierre; or, The Ambiguities*, music emerges as an alternative form of expression. At the time, music was considered the ideal human expression, the means by which to achieve the most perfect and profound philosophical utterance. More than just thematizing *Pierre; or, The Ambiguities*, certain passages in the work reflect Melville's own fraught relationship with the written word as a mode of expression. Melville's struggle with the process of writing also displays his difficulty with expressing truth via language. Melville envisioned *Pierre; or, The Ambiguities* as a work which, like *Moby-Dick*, would continue along a truth-seeking path. From the outset of *Pierre; or, The Ambiguities*, Melville believed in seeking and uttering truths, even if he felt they existed beyond the written word. It is

---

① Thwaites S. "'Mirror with a Memory': Theories of Light and Preternatural Negatives in Herman Melville's *Moby-Dick*". European Journal of American Culture, 2013, 32(2): 121-136.

② Duban J. "Narrative Self-Absolution and Political Tyranny in *Moby-Dick* and *Darkness at Noon*". Papers on Language and Literature, 2018, 54(3): 237-260.

precisely at this nexus of linguistic suspicion and yet never failing faith that human expression could somehow approach and ultimately reveal philosophical profundities that so much of Dwight's music theory hinged upon.①

John Haydock, in "Melville and Balzac: The Man in Cream-Colors", offers a definite example of Herman Melville's still widely unacknowledged dependence on French author Honoré de Balzac for devising his narrative structures, ontology, and scheme of characterization. After demonstrating that Melville had ample opportunity to have experienced significant awareness and analysis of Balzac's massive *La Comédie humaine* by 1857, the author compares specific narrative and linguistic elements between Balzac's *Christ in Flanders* and Melville's *The Confidence-Man* to demonstrate the extent of this reliance. In the process, the essay offers an explanation for several unanswered questions about the novel, particularly the meaning of the inserted critical chapters on original characters, the ontological nature of the satiric tale, and the ferryboat resetting of what has assumed to have been inspired by an urban incident. The article concludes that it was Balzac's influence and achievement that drove Melville throughout his career to attempt to create a sociological corpus of American literature.②

8. Marxism Study

Robert Tally, in "*Herman Melville: Between Charlemagne and the Antemosaic Cosmic Man: Race, Class, and the Crisis of Bourgeois Ideology in the American Renaissance Writer*", reviews Loren Goldner's *Herman Melville: Between*

---

① McClendon A. "'For not in Words Can It Be Spoken': John Sullivan Dwight's Transcendental Music Theory and Herman Melville's *Pierre; or, The Ambiguities*". American Transcendental Quarterly, 2005, 19(1): 23-36.

② Haydock J. "Melville and Balzac: The Man in Cream-Colors". College Literature, 2008, 35(1): 58-81.

Charlemagne and the Antemosaic Cosmic Man, which posits that Melville was the American Marx, exposing the crisis of bourgeois ideology in the revolutionary period around 1848. Goldner follows a tradition of Marxian scholarship of Melville, notably including C. L. R. James, Michael Paul Rogin, and Cesare Casarino. Tally concludes that Goldner's argument, while interesting, is limited by its focus on American exceptionalism and by ignoring the postnational force of Melville's novels. ①

Rick Mitchell, in "*The Confidence Man*: Performing the Magic of Modernity", argues that Herman Melville appropriated the confidence man, a uniquely American figure, for his 1857 novel *The Confidence Man*. Eschewing established conventions of realism, Melville wrote a seemingly impenetrable novel which both enacts and subverts the rapidly intensifying commodification of experience in mid-nineteenth-century America. Published while Karl Marx was beginning to develop his theory of the fetishism of commodities in his private notebooks, *The Confidence Man* uncannily embodies and critiques the magical nature of the commodity, as well as the often deceptive (though necessary) trait upon which commodity exchange is so dependent: confidence. ②

9. Traumatic Study

William Brevda, in "*Moby Dick*: A Nasty Night for Hats and Men", argues that Herman Melville's interest in hats derives from his boyhood trauma when his father went bankrupt and Herman Melville was forced to drop out of school. Haunted

---

① Tally R. "*Herman Melville*: Between Charlemagne and the Antemosaic Cosmic Man: Race, Class, and the Crisis of Bourgeois Ideology in the American Renaissance Writer". Historical Materialism, 2009, 17 (3): 235-243.

② Mitchell R. "*The Confidence Man*: Performing the Magic of Modernity". European Journal of American Culture, 2004, 23(1): 51-62.

by his father's disgrace and death, and by his own Bartleby-like experience as a clerk in a haberdashery for almost two years, Herman Melville had personal reasons for associating the loss of manhood with the loss of a hat. In *Moby Dick*, Herman Melville expressed his feelings of abandonment and resentment through the symbolism of hats. [①]

10. Post-colonial Study

Helen Lock, in "The Paradox of Slave Mutiny in Herman Melville, Charles Johnson, and Frederick Douglass", argues that Melville's *Benito Cereno* is a problematic text that students of color, especially, can find troubling. However, when this story is studied alongside two other narratives of shipboard slave rebellions—Charles Johnson's *Middle Passage* and Frederick Douglass's *The Heroic Slave*—it becomes apparent that Melville is making the same point as these writers about such rebellions, through the subtle use of paradox as the key rhetorical strategy. In these texts, not only are slave mutinies seen as inherently paradoxical, but so is the status quo that the mutinies seemingly invert, so that mutineers and officers, slave and fee, are revealed to be two sides of the same coin—ultimately they are each other. By foregrounding inconsistencies, the use of paradox serves to undermine and invert apparent fixed verities, and then reveals beneath them the organic interdependence of the mirror and its image. Those involved in the rebellions described by Melville, Johnson, and Douglass usually fail to realize this, however, like Narcissus, they cannot recognize the inverted image as themselves. This interdependence, in *Benito Cereno* especially, is therefore found in the story's subtext: Melville's covert means of making a subversive point. Such use of paradox

---

① Brevda W. "*Moby Dick*: A Nasty Night for Hats and Men". Texas Studies in Literature and Language, 2017, 59(4): 421-456.

is in fact broadly characteristic of the slave-mutiny narrative genre as a whole, providing a useful approach for studying all such texts. ①

Nasser Maleki and Mohammad Javad Haj'jari, in "Melville's *Typee* as a Portrait of Colonial Representation", argue that travel narrative is an omnipresent mode of cultural representation among nations, whose manipulation by colonial powers in representing the colonized has shed light on specific facts about the lives of both the parties, in either subjective or objective ways. Herman Melville's *Typee* oscillates between a purely objective description of native islanders and a subjective colonial representation from the viewpoint of a white explorer in exotic lands. Melville's contribution to colonial travel narratives presents a series of events which deny the ability of the colonial gaze to visually possess exotic lands and its indigenous people through colonial supervision and control, and thus signifies Tommo's inability to assign real significance to Typees and their land. The travel narrative genre itself gives Melville the license to present otherwise than the convention. ②

Bryce Traister, in "Terrorism before the Letter: *Benito Cereno* and the *9/11 Commission Report*", argues that Herman Melville's 1855 novella, *Benito Cereno*, serves as a historical model for thinking through the construction of paranoid narrative in the *9/11 Commission Report*. Melville's text invites a consideration of slavery's role in the preservation of status quo politics, and reveals the means by which the disclosure of secrecy becomes a condition for the legal fiction of slavery to persist. In purporting to reveal the hidden plot of contemporary anti-US terrorism, the US government's *9/11 Commission Report* similarly manufactures an acceptable political fiction that compensates for a still deeper failure to promote democratic structures of feeling in response to national trauma. ③

---

① Lock H. "The Paradox of Slave Mutiny in Herman Melville, Charles Johnson, and Frederick Douglass". College Literature, 2003, 30(4): 54-70.

② Maleki N, Haj'jari M J. "Melville's *Typee* as a Portrait of Colonial Representation". Coldnoon: Travel Poetics, 2018, 6(5): 82-110.

③ Traister B. "Terrorism before the Letter: *Benito Cereno* and the *9/11 Commission Report*". Canadian Review of American Studies, 2013, 43(1): 23-47.

11. Religious Study

Justin Saxby, in "Toadstools, Bartleby, and Badiou", brings together Herman Melville's *Bartleby, the Scrivener* with *The Lives of Jesus* authored by David Strauss and Simon Greenleaf, and reads them through Alain Badiou's philosophy of the Event. If we bear in mind the raging debates of the time about how to write an historical account of Jesus, represented here by Strauss and Greenleaf, Melville's story about a reclusive law-copyist and his frustrated biographer becomes a set of questions about the nature and purpose of biography. When Badiou's ideas about the Event are taken into account, Bartleby intensifies into an anguished consideration of what to do, or what to write, after a life-altering encounter with an elusive subject who leaves no evidentiary trace. [1]

12. Social Study

Debra J. Rosenthal, in "The Sentimental Appeal to Salvific Paternity in *Uncle Tom's Cabin* and *Moby-Dick*", presents critiques of the influences of Harriet Beecher Stowe's *Uncle Tom's Cabin* and Herman Melville's *Moby-Dick*, which represents to different issues in the world. It explores the themes of the novels, focusing on topics including the international progressive social reform, seafaring men and religious exhortations. The author also discusses the relationships of pre-industrial whaling between whales and whalers. [2]

---

[1] Saxby J. "Toadstools, Bartleby, and Badiou". Religion and the Arts, 2015, 19(1/2): 51-73.
[2] Rosenthal D J. "The Sentimental Appeal to Salvific Paternity in *Uncle Tom's Cabin* and *Moby-Dick*". Texas Studies in Literature and Language, 2014, 56(2): 135-147.

Chapter 4　Herman Melville

Benjamin S. West, in "The Work of Redburn: Melville's Critique of Capitalism", presents literary criticism of the book *Redburn* by Herman Melville. The author suggests that the book, a bildungsroman about the travels of the character Redburn, is a criticism of capitalism. The novel's themes of socioeconomic status, exploitation of the poor, and ocean voyages are discussed. The character Redburn is examined for his naïveté, poor social status, and romanticized understanding of the concept of the American dream. [1]

Philip Loosemore, in "Revolution, Counterrevolution, and Natural Law in *Billy Budd, Sailor*", offers literary criticism of the book *Billy Budd, Sailor* by Herman Melville. Themes of mutiny, revolutionary radicalism, and British monarchial authority are explored within the novella, along with Melville's use of the character Billy Budd to comment on his thoughts regarding the rights of man. [2]

---

[1] West B S. "The Work of Redburn: Melville's Critique of Capitalism". The Midwest Quarterly, 2011, 52(2): 165-181.

[2] Loosemore P. "Revolution, Counterrevolution, and Natural Law in *Billy Budd, Sailor*". Criticism, 2011, 53(1): 99-126.

Chapter 5

Edgar Allan Poe

Edgar Allan Poe(1809-1849)

Poe classified his own fiction into the categories of "Tales of the Grotesque and Arabesque". Borrowing these terms from Scott, Poe meant by them to describe satirical, bizarre, and jocose writings on the one hand, and on the other the fictional equivalents of poems. These were his prose efforts to excite his readers souls by the contemplation of beauty and terror. His review of Hawthorne outlines his theory of fiction. The tale, like the poem, must be all of a place, each detail contributing to the desired unity of effect; symbolism must be present as a profound undercurrent in the tale. His fiction will work by indirection.

Critical Perspectives

1. Psychoanalytical Study

Pelin Dogan, in "The Uncanny as the Intrasubjectivity in the (m)Other: Edgar Allan Poe's *Morella*", investigates the contribution of the sense of the uncanny to the intensification of mystery in Edgar Allan Poe's short story titled "Morella", using Freudian ideas as a backcloth. This paper aims to look at how Poe makes use of the psychodynamics of the characters at the intersection of the (m)other, death and the uncanny. In this sense, typical of Poesque literature is that his work is marked by tales of horror, mystery, the macabre, and morbid imagery; the sense of the uncanny is an indispensable part of a plotline which includes semantic loopholes and narrative ruptures. The unnamed male narrator of the story offers a retrospective account of his past memories from his marriage to Morella up to the death of his daughter, which reveals that this unreliable narrator suffers from a psychic regression by establishing intrasubjectivity with his wife. Using Freudian epistemology, this paper also discusses the ways in which how the mysterious bond established between this couple generates its uncanny effect. Such a reading of the short story is especially useful because although much has been written on Poe's representation of women and death, this paper aims to open up a discursive space to discuss the operations of the psychodynamics of characters within the framework of the Freudian uncanny, which has not received adequate scholarly attention from psychoanalytic circles.①

John Samuel Tieman, in "Sergeant Major Edgar Allan Poe", frames Edgar Allan Poe's history as an enlisted man in the United States army. For Poe, these were years of accomplishments as both artist and soldier. When researching this article, two forms of comment are readily detected. Military historians immediately understand the significance in Poe's meteoric rise to sergeant major. But these writers tend not to appreciate the literary history. Literary historians often note that Poe was an enlisted soldier, but, beyond that, seem not to appreciate that information. In none of this is there any sense that Poe sought, and for two years found, a degree of emotional stability. The social structure of the army contained and maintained Poe's psychic structure. This intertwining of the military and the literary, coupled with an understanding of psycho-social development, is the frame needed to understand Sergeant Major Poe.②

Jeffrey Folks, in "Edgar Allan Poe and Elias Canetti: Illuminating the Sources of Terror", discusses the concept of fear and isolation in the writings of author Edgar Allan Poe and Elias Canetti. Topics discussed include similarity of the writings of Canetti with Poe; discussion of the patterns of crowd behavior in the book *Crowds and Power*, by Canetti; and elements in the works of Poe that were observed by Canetti.③

Carrie Zlotnick-Woldenberg, in "Edgar Allan Poe's *Ligeia*: An Object-Relational Interpretation", argues that Poe's short story *Ligeia*, in which the narrator experiences the death of his adored first wife (Ligeia), a second marriage

---

① Dogan P. "The Uncanny as the Intrasubjectivity in the (m)Other: Edgar Allan Poe's *Morella*". Gaziantep University Journal of Social Sciences, 2021, 20(1): 125-135.

② Tieman J S. "Sergeant Major Edgar Allan Poe". International Journal of Applied Psychoanalytic Studies, 2016, 13(4): 351-366.

③ Folks J. "Edgar Allan Poe and Elias Canetti: Illuminating the Sources of Terror". The Southern Literary Journal, 2005, 37(2): 1-16.

to the despised Rowena, and ultimately the death of Rowena and the revivification of Ligeia, is not a supernatural tale, but rather a psychological one. According to this reading, the poisoning of Rowena and the revivification of Ligeia are hallucinated by the narrator in the course of an opium-induced psychotic break. The antecedents to this break are explored in light of object relations theory, with particular emphasis placed on the way in which the two women function as part objects. Ligeia represents the narrator's romantic and spiritual side, and is associated with the good mother, while Rowena, who represents his more mundane and materialistic side, is associated with the rejecting mother. It is argued that the narrator, functioning primarily in the schizoid position and employing suck defense mechanisms as splitting and projection—which already require a high degree of fantasy—is not an unlikely candidate for suck a break. [1]

Lorelei Caraman, in "Poe's *The Gold-Bug*: From the Reading of Madness to the Madness of Its Readings", seeks to establish a relationship between the scene of reading within Poe's tale and the scene of the tale's early psychoanalytic readings. By first following the function of interpretation within the text and subsequently moving to some of the characteristics of its critical interpretations, this essay aims to show how *The Gold-Bug*, not only anticipates its misreadings, but also deconstructs them ultimately. One of the paper's main objectives, therefore, is to bring into the foreground what Pierre Bayard calls "the paradoxical nature" of the literary text, by illustrating the way in which Poe's short story invites a reading of madness, while simultaneously exposing the "madness" of its readings. [2]

Joseph Church, in "'To Make Venus Vanish': Misogyny as Motive in Poe's *Murders in the Rue Morgue*", considers misogyny as motive in the short story

---

[1] Zlotnick-Woldenberg C. "Edgar Allan Poe's *Ligeia*: An Object-Relational Interpretation". American Journal of Psychotherapy, 1999, 53(3): 403-412.

[2] Caraman L. "Poe's *The Gold-Bug*: From the Reading of Madness to the Madness of Its Readings". Philologica Jassyensia, 2014, 1(19): 131-138.

Murders in the Rue Morgue, by Edgar Allan Poe. The story describes the motiveless deaths of a Parisian mother and daughter who have baffled the police until Auguste Dupin solves the crimes by deducing and demonstrating that a sailor's escaped orangutan has carried out the carnage. Poe suggests that Dupin risks and resists association with internal feminity. The story identifies Dupin with the orangutan and associates the animal with androgyny. ①

2. Gender Study

Katherine J. Kim, in "Horrifying Obsession: Reading Incest in Edgar Allan Poe's *Ligeia*", examines American author Edgar Allan Poe's short story *Ligeia* (first published in 1838) through the lenses of sibling and other forms of incest in the first half of the nineteenth century along with more recent knowledge regarding incest and its ramifications. Research into legal documents, newspapers, magazines, literature, and other written works from around Poe's lifetime reveal social, scientific, and cultural tensions regarding "appropriate" levels of incest and the usage of opposite-sex siblings as templates for future erotic love. Although other works by Poe, such as *The Fall of the House of Usher* (1839), have previously been evaluated for references to incest and its resultant trauma, *Ligeia* has not been considered in this manner. Despite such exclusion, the undertones of sibling incest in *Ligeia* serve to enhance Poe's strategic development of horror in the reader by merging ambiguity with a reflection of late-eighteenth-century and nineteenth-century shifting sentiments on incest stemming from previously sanctioned familial

---

① Church J. "'To Make Venus Vanish': Misogyny as Motive in Poe's *Murders in the Rue Morgue*". American Transcendental Quarterly, 2006, 20(2): 407-418.

attachments that precluded idealized romantic love.①

David Greven, in "Valdemar's Abjection: Poe, Kristeva, Masculinity, and Victim-Monsters", explores intersections between Edgar Allan Poe's 1845 tale *The Facts in the Case of M. Valdemar* and Julia Kristeva's *Powers of Horror: An Essay on Abjection* (1982). Highly influential, Kristeva's work illuminates Poe's depiction of a man mesmerized on the point of death, his vibrating tongue the only indication of life. In his liminal condition between life and death, Valdemar transforms into a spectacle witnessed over time by a male group whose members remain intimately tied to yet always distant and aloof from him. As a spectacle of body horror, Valdemar evokes many of the attributes of Kristevan abjection theory, especially the fluids and waste materials associated with the maternal body. Challenging the maternal focus of abjection theory and its reception, this essay tracks the ways in which Poe's tale locates abject affect in the fears of the male body and in the male group's relationship to the expulsed, isolate male. Another antebellum author, the health reformer Sylvester Graham, provides a striking point of comparison in his focus on the young male onanist. Through Kristeva's and Poe's works, this essay develops a theory of the victim-monster, a being whose suffering initially incites sympathy but ultimately repels the spectator; the victim becomes monstrous. The victim-monster of Poe's tale intersects with the figure of the grotesque and anti-Semitic caricature.②

3. Narrative Study

Harry Lee Poe, in "Creating a Medium for Exploring the Implications of

---

① Kim K J. "Horrifying Obsession: Reading Incest in Edgar Allan Poe's *Ligeia*". Sexuality & Culture, 2021, 25(3): 960-980.

② Greven D. "Valdemar's Abjection: Poe, Kristeva, Masculinity, and Victim-Monsters". Studies in Gender and Sexuality, 2018, 19(3): 191-203.

Science: Edgar Allan Poe and the First Science Fiction", argues that science fiction has emerged as one of our culture's means of carrying on a broader conversation about the direction of both science and technology. It asks the questions of unintended consequences and what might be the long-term outcome of applied science. One of the first writers to develop this new genre was Edgar Allan Poe. In fact, it is in his writings that we find the first examples of many of the plots that still embody science fiction today. ①

Brenda Tyrrell, in "A World Turned upside down: *Hop-Frog*, Freak Shows, and Representations of Dwarfism", considers Edgar Allan Poe's *Hop-Frog* and *American Horror Story: Freak Show* in order to determine how and if any change in the portrayal of dwarfism occurs in the time between the publication of the two texts. First, the article touches on the rise and fall of the freak show, followed by a brief history of dwarfism. Next, a short discussion of several key concepts is undertaken before beginning a close examination of the characters identified as dwarfs in both works. Last, the article analyzes the similarities and differences between the two texts and considers what is at stake in the larger picture of the lived experiences of dwarfs through the concept of "cripping up". ②

Jang Ki Yoon, in "Edgar Allan Poe and the Author-Fiction: *The Narrative of Arthur Gordon Pym of Nantucket*", considers that author Edgar Allan Poe is reader-oriented and reader-inviting. It relies on the fact that Poe wrote under the 19th century American magazine culture that an author must be read to be appreciated. It cites his novel *The Narrative of Arthur Gordon Pym of Nantucket*, which showed his awareness and search for a kind of author-figure and author-reader relationship. It indicates that Poe's authorship should be understood as heteronomous and self-

---

① Poe H L. "Creating a Medium for Exploring the Implications of Science: Edgar Allan Poe and the First Science Fiction". Perspectives on Science and Christian Faith, 2017, 69(2): 76-86.

② Tyrrell B. "A World Turned upside down: *Hop-Frog*, Freak Shows, and Representations of Dwarfism". Journal of Literary and Cultural Disability Studies, 2020, 14(2): 171-186.

dispossessing, and calls for reconsideration and modification of one's perception of Poe. ①

Vanessa Warne, in "'If You Should Ever Want an Arm': Disability and Dependency in Edgar Allan Poe's *The Man that Was Used up*", analyzes the representation of disability in Edgar Allan Poe's short story *The Man that Was Used up*. Topics discussed include political interpretation of Poe's description of a war hero; contention on how Poe used the wounded body of the General to explore and express a range of anxieties about disability and dependency; and consideration of Poe's commentary on progress as an expression of his sometimes troubled relationship with literary innovation and changing public taste. ②

4. Reader-response Study

Maggie Tonkin, in "The 'Poe-etics' of Decomposition: Angela Carter's *The Cabinet of Edgar Allan Poe* and the Reading-Effect", argues that few authors are as undead as Edgar Allan Poe. Despite having been interred over 150 years ago, Poe continues to generate effects. In *The Philosophy of Composition*, he claimed to meticulously calculate his effects, to write, so to speak, from the effect backwards. His notorious statement that "death, then, of a beautiful woman is, unquestionably, the most poetical topic in the world" ought to be read as a calculated, attempt at achieving a certain preconceived effect. But, despite his claims of being calculating, Poe could not have foreseen the discursive effects his work would generate. He remains one of the most controversial figures in American

---

① Yoon J K. "Edgar Allan Poe and the Author-Fiction: *The Narrative of Arthur Gordon Pym of Nantucket*". Texas Studies in Literature and Language, 2010, 52(4): 355-380.

② Warne V. "'If You Should Ever Want an Arm': Disability and Dependency in Edgar Allan Poe's *The Man that Was Used up*". Atenea, 2005, 25(1): 95-105.

literature, a writer whose status is always in dispute. [1]

Darlene Harbour Unrue, in "Edgar Allan Poe: The Romantic as Classicist", argues that Edgar Allan Poe's affinity with classical values has not been properly noted by critics and other readers who have interpreted the romantic and Gothic elements in his fiction and poetry as proof of Poe's predilection for the subjective, macabre, and fantastic, as well as the transcendental. A careful examination of Poe's use of seemingly romantic materials, however, reveals that he measured the romantic stance detrimentally against the objectivity and rationality of the classical. Poe drew allusion and structure from his reading of classical literature to inform his own works with a classical worldview he sought in both life and art. [2]

5. Religious Study

Jonathan A. Cook, in "Poe and the Apocalyptic Sublime: *The Masque of the Red Death*", examines *The Masque of the Read Death*, one of Poe's most allusive tales, as a striking example of the aesthetics of the apocalyptic sublime. Combining several key ideas from Edmund Burke's *A Philosophical Enquiry into the Origin of Our Ideas of the Sublime and Beautiful* with numerous motifs from biblical apocalyptic symbolism, Poe's *Masque* was specifically designed to create an effect of sublime terror in the reader. Basing his image of mass death on the cholera pandemic of 1832, which killed thousands of individuals in Europe and America, Poe created a historically grounded parable of apocalyptic extinction with a myriad of connections with literary, biblical, and artistic tradition. Poe's tale echoes many

---

[1] Tonkin M. "The 'Poe-etics' of Decomposition: Angela Carter's *The Cabinet of Edgar Allan Poe and the Reading-Effect*". Women's Studies, 2004, 33(1): 1-21.

[2] Unrue D H. "Edgar Allan Poe: The Romantic as Classicist". International Journal of the Classical Tradition, 1995, 1(4): 112-119.

of Burke's remarks on the nature and sources of sublime and beautiful effects while conveying a biblically based vision of human mortality. ①

Donald W. Olson and Shaun B. Ford, in "The Comets of Edgar Allan Poe", focus on the fascination of writer and poet Edgar Allan Poe with astronomy, focusing on his astronomical references throughout his work. Topics include his 1848 nonfiction work *Eureka* that focuses on physical cosmology, with particular consideration on the passages of Poe regarding Earth's atmosphere derived from *The Christian Philosopher*, by Thomas Dick, *The Geography of the Heavens*, by Elijah Burritt, and *A Treatise on Astronomy*, by John Herschel. ②

Codrin Liviu Cutitaru, in "The Art of Dissimulation. The Good Christian vs. the Loyal Freemason", focuses on one of Edgar Allan Poe's famous tales, *The Cask of Amontillado*, a story of "perfect crime", as it is usually considered. The action is set in medieval Italy, at the time of the Carnival, in Venice. The protagonists are two noblemen, Montresor and Fortunado. Montresor is the narrator of the text and wants to revenge on Fortunado, because of a mysterious "insult". Fortunado's "mistake" is never made clear, although the punishment for the trespassing as such is extreme (Fortunado eventually pays with his own life). The article tries to explain the enigma behind the "insult". This takes readers into an occult world, where the identities of the characters change dramatically (they are, successively, social competitors, religious enemies and rival Masons). Poe's symbolism and epic games become here remarkable tools of constructing and amplifying the mystery. *The Cask of Amontillado* should therefore be viewed as a

---

① Cook J A. "Poe and the Apocalyptic Sublime: *The Masque of the Red Death*". Religion and the Arts, 2019, 23(5): 489-515.

② Olson D W, Ford S B. "The Comets of Edgar Allan Poe". Sky and Telescope, 2016, 132(6): 30-35.

masterpiece of the American Romanticism and of "horror genre" as well. ①

Jeffrey Einboden, in "The Early American Qur'an: Islamic Scripture and US Canon", argues that although considerable scholarly attention has been paid to US Orientalism in the nineteenth century, there remains no targeted study of the formative influence exercised by the Qur'an upon the canon of early American literature. The paper surveys receptions, adaptations and translations of the Qur'an during the American Renaissance, identifying the Qur'anic echoes which permeate the seminal works of literary patriarchs such as Ralph Waldo Emerson, Washington Irving and Edgar Allan Poe. Examining the literary and religious tensions raised by antebellum importations of Islamic scripture, the essay interrogates how the aesthetic contours of the Qur'an in particular serve both to attract and obstruct early US readings, mapping the diverse responses to the Muslim sacred generated by American Romantics and Transcendentalists. ②

6. Canonization Study

Irmgard Schopen, in "Poe on the Veld: Herman Charles Bosman's Use of Edgar Allan Poe as a Literary Model", discusses the influence of American writer Edgar Allan Poe on South African writer Herman Charles Bosman's writings. Topics discussed include comparison of Poe and Bosman; Bosman's development as a writer; Bosman's response to Poe's literary criticism; role of American literary studies in South Africa; and question of comparison. ③

---

① Cutitaru C L. "The Art of Dissimulation. The Good Christian vs. the Loyal Freemason". Philologica Jassyensia, 2017, 13(2): 203-209.
② Einboden J. "The Early American Qur'an: Islamic Scripture and US Canon". Journal of Qur'anic Studies, 2009, 11(2): 1-19.
③ Schopen I. "Poe on the Veld: Herman Charles Bosman's Use of Edgar Allan Poe as a Literary Model". American Studies International, 1993, 31(2): 82-88.

Burton R. Pollin, in "Kilmer's Promotion of Poe", presents the poet Joyce Kilmer and his respect for crime writing pioneer Edgar Allan Poe. Excerpts from his interviews and essays are presented. Various letters exchanged between Poe and members of the New York City literary community are also offered. As editor of *The New York Times*, Kilmer was able to promote, and in a way, sculpt, the popularity of Poe as a literary figure. [1]

7. Biological Study

Philip Beidler, in "Soldier Poe", presents an examination into the military life of the 19th-century American author Edgar Allan Poe. Introductory details are given noting that not only did Poe serve multiple years as a soldier in the U.S. army, but that it also served as a highly influential period of his life. Accounts are given to describe his years of service after pressure from his guardian John Allan, including training at the West Point Military Academy, the challenges he faced within the disciplined and authoritative lifestyle, and his reputation for drunkenness. [2]

8. Philosophical Study

Jeffrey Folks, in "Poe and the 'Cogito'", discusses the evaluation of Edgar Allan Poe on the implications of Rene Descartes' "Cognito". It states that the writings of Poe emphasizes the distinction between essence and existence, and the recurring sense of the insubstantiality of the physical world. It notes that Poe has suggested that the ability of mind to perceive an existing order of certainty is a proof

---

[1] Pollin B R. "Kilmer's Promotion of Poe". The Southern Quarterly, 2006, 44(1): 120-150.
[2] Beidler P. "Soldier Poe". The Midwest Quarterly, 2012, 53(4): 329-343.

of transcendent order. It emphasizes that Poe does not resort to the rationalistic force of the "Cognito" to resolve problems, unlike Descartes. ①

9. Ethical Study

Magdalen Wing-Chi Ki, in "Diabolical Evil and *The Black Cat*", discusses diabolical evil as expressed in American author Edgar Allan Poe's short story *The Black Cat*. Most critics believe that Poe's story is about the anatomy of an evil mind rather than about morality or ethics. One critic believes that even though Poe's works are full of ethical content, he writes with psychology in mind rather than ethics. This article argues that *The Black Cat* is basically ethical. ②

---

① Folks J. "Poe and the 'Cogito'". The Southern Literary Journal, 2009, 42(1): 57-72.
② Ki M W-C. "Diabolical Evil and *The Black Cat*". Mississippi Quarterly, 2009, 62(4): 569-589.

Chapter 6

William Dean Howells

William Dean Howells (1837-1920)

William Dean Howell's literary career was remarkable not only for its length and variousness, but for its continuous and conscientious productivity. For more than fifty years, extending from the 19th century into the 20th century, Howells appeared in print as a journalist, a pet, a sensitively observant but unsentimental traveler, a novelist, a playwright, a critic and a polemicist in the cause of realism, a publicist and explicator of foreign writers for an ill-informed American public, and the educator of that same public to the greatness of its own writers like James and Twain.

Critical Perspectives

1. Thematic Study

Wai-Chee Dimock, in "The Economy of Pain: The Case of Howells", presents the most touching moments in William Dean Howell's novel *The Rise of Silas Lapham*, where the Laphams, feeling wretched about the drastic development in their daughters' marital fortunes, consult the Reverend Sewell. Topics discussed include Sewell's economy of pain; how suffering can become morally acceptable, according to Sewell; importance of Howell's remarks; and why the grounds for equivalence in *The Rise of Silas Lapham* are interesting. [1]

2. New-historicism

Samantha Bernstein, in "The Joys of the Elevated: William Dean Howells and the Urban Picturesque", examines picturesque aesthetics in nineteenth-century American realism as an expression of unease about middle-class life and as a manifestation of liberal guilt. Previous scholarship on the picturesque in American literature sees it as the failure of middle-class writers to represent urban poverty. The author of this essay demonstrates the historical association of the picturesque with the formation of the middle class and argues that, since the eighteenth century, picturesque aesthetics have played a significant role in discourse about class

---

[1] Dimock W-C. "The Economy of Pain: The Case of Howells". Raritan, 1990, 9 (4): 99.

relations. Through a reading of William Dean Howells's *A Hazard of New Fortunes*, the author examines the picturesque as a means of addressing the ethical dilemmas of liberal humanists, whose compassion for the poor is undermined by a sense of its ineffectuality. Picturesque aesthetics are culturally significant today, suggesting a need to examine their social and ethical implications. [1]

3. Gender Study

Patricia J. Sehulster, in "The Unanswerable Woman Question in William Dean Howells's *A Hazard of New Fortunes*", claims that the female characters in the novel *A Hazard of New Fortunes*, by William Dean Howells, represent some aspects of unanswerable nature of the woman question and the negative effects of grasping any one of the possible roles of womanhood. Perhaps the most telling effects surface in the characters of Elizabeth Dryfoos, Isabel March, Christine Dryfoos, Alma Leighton, and Miss Woodburn. Together these women represent the multi-faceted, confusing, and conflicted microcosm of American female society. Howells says that each man serves as a microcosm, and the writer who can acquaint the reader ultimately with half a dozen people has done something which no one can call narrow. Howell's *A Hazard of New Fortunes* epitomizes this theory, for its story portrays several different microcosms of society, each small group comprising a membership that together represents some segment of late nineteenth-century American life. As a realist and an American, Howells presents a debate with the conventions of outdated romance and competing versions of reality. The women of *A Hazard of New Fortunes* become very much a part of that portrayal. Each female character embodies a different element of those competing visions, and as Howells

---

[1] Bernstein S. "The Joys of the Elevated: William Dean Howells and the Urban Picturesque". Canadian Review of American Studies, 2015, 45(3): 278-299.

contemplates the problem of showing a society composed of competing and seemingly mutually exclusive realities, he conveys the ineffectiveness of each one. In analyzing *A Hazard of New fortunes*, most scholars, including Amy Kaplan, Alfred Habegger, Allen F. Stein, Christopher Diller, Susanna Ashton, and John Crowley, focus on the competing contingencies of the real world and the romantic one, the labor market and the commercial world, the artistic realm and the materialistic one, the family and the larger society, or even the female sphere and the male one, but few examine the competing realities of the woman's world alone. [1]

4. Narrative Study

Linnie Blake, in "William Dean Howells and the City of New York: A Hazard of New Writing", focuses on the development of urban writing as reflected in the works of William Dean Howells. Formal and thematic changes in Howells' writings in the last years of the nineteenth century demonstrated the shift from the stasis of the rural past to the transient modern city of the present. The article also examines how Howells depicted the changes in life, artistic apprehension and literary representation prompted by capitalism. Howells also illustrated how money underwrote and framed the disjunctive, fragmented aspects of urban life. [2]

Patricia Howe, in "William Dean Howells's *Indian Summer* and Theodor Fontane's *Effi Briest*: Forms and Phases of the Realist Novel", argues that reviewing Fontane's essay on William Dean Howells's novel *A Foregone Conclusion*, Werner Hoffmeister identifies parallels in the two writers' careers and

---

[1] Sehulster P J. "The Unanswerable Woman Question in William Dean Howells's *A Hazard of New Fortunes*". American Transcendental Quarterly, 2005, 19(2):115-131.

[2] Blake L. "William Dean Howells and the City of New York: A Hazard of New Writing". Studies in the Literary Imagination, 2008, 41(1): 1-19.

in their thinking about the realist novel. Building on Hoffmeister's suggestion that a comparison of individual novels would be fruitful, this essay compares Howells's novel *Indian Summer* and Fontane's *Effi Briest*. It suggests a more differentiated relationship between their conceptions of realism, showing how the realist's illusion of truth and plausibility produce distinct and variable forms of stylization, which are, at least in part, responses to cultural contexts. [1]

Edward J. Piacentino, in "Arms in Love and War in Howells' *Editha*", focuses on the short story *Editha*, written by William Dean Howells. Topics discussed include use of arm imagery throughout the book; phrases containing references to arms in the context of war and military activities; influence of George Bernard Shaw's *Arms and the Man* on the short story; and significance of the introduction of arm images at strategic points in the narrative. [2]

5. Religious Study

Thomas Wortham, in "William Dean Howells's Spiritual Quest(ioning) in a 'World Come of Age'", presents an essay on the multi-dimensional view of 19th American literature realist William Dean Howells. This essay, which focuses on Howells' struggles with belief, benefits from those decades' labor. Howells belong to an American generation along with Emily Dickinson, Mark Twain, and William James. His questioning of the meaning and consequences of Christian faith is highlighted. The references and echoes of the Bible in his works are noted. [3]

---

[1] Howe P. "William Dean Howells's *Indian Summer* and Theodor Fontane's *Effi Briest*: Forms and Phases of the Realist Novel". Modern Language Review, 2007, 102(1): 125-138.

[2] Piacentino E J. "Arms in Love and War in Howells' *Editha*". Studies in Short Fiction, 1987, 24(4): 425-432.

[3] Wortham T. "William Dean Howells's Spiritual Quest(ioning) in a 'World Come of Age'". Renascence, 2013, 65(3): 206-224.

6. Canonization Study

Renata Wasserman, in "The Press in Novels: Credit, Power, and Mobility in William D. Howells's *Modern Instance* and Lima Barreto's *Recordações do Escrivão Isaías Caminha*", discusses the similarities of the novels *A Modern Instance* by William D. Howells and *Recordações do Escrivão Isaías Caminha* by Lima Barreto. She examines how the two novels have attracted public scrutiny and discussion about the relationship of economics, truth, and life events. The author recalls both the author's dissimilar careers as well as the history of the press in the two environments where they wrote.[1]

7. Biological Study

Stephen Miller, in "Loathing & Loving New York", discusses the views of writers such as Walt Whitman, Henry James, and Lydia Child in regards to New York City, focusing on the attitudes of the author William Dean Howells to New York City over the course of his career. Topics include Howells' novel *A Hazard of New Fortunes*, the fictional character Basil March, comparisons between New York City and Boston, Massachusetts, and Howells' response to the 1886 Haymarket Riot in Chicago, Illinois.[2]

Keith Newlin, in "'I Am as Ever Your Disciple': The Friendship of Hamlin Garland and W. D. Howells", provides an overview of the friendship of authors

---

[1] Wasserman R. "The Press in Novels: Credit, Power, and Mobility in William D. Howells's *Modern Instance* and Lima Barreto's *Recordações do Escrivão Isaías Caminha*". Comparative Literature Studies, 2011, 48(1): 44-63.

[2] Miller S. "Loathing & Loving New York". The New Criterion, 2014, 32(6): 20-26.

Hamlin Garland and William Dean Howells. Garland had first learned of Howells in 1881 when he bought from a shopkeeper a second-copy of the book *The Undiscovered Country*, by Howell. Garland and Howells formally met in 1887 in Auburndale, Massachusetts. Over the years, Howells greatly aided Garland's career, while Garland has drawn all the assistance Howells cared to offer on his ambition to become a writer. ①

William H. Pritchard, in "Howells and the Right American Stuff", examines the significance of novelist William Dean Howells in the American literature. It focuses on Lionel Trilling's special interest in the cultural implications and achievement of an individual writer, but does not direct to the specific things in Howell's art. It discusses the essays of Henry James devoted to Howells which describes Howells' central characteristics as a novelist. It cites the predominant note of romance on Howell's novel. ②

8. Philosophical Study

James E. Smethurst, in "Paul Laurence Dunbar and Turn-into-the-20th-Century African American Dualism", examines the contribution of African American poet Paul Laurence Dunbar to African American dualism in the 20th century. In dualism, its problem lies in being a citizen and yet not a citizen in an increasingly urbanized and industrialized U.S. There are speculations on how to respond, whether through integration or separatism. Dunbar has the notion of masking one's

---

① Newlin K. "'I Am as Ever Your Disciple': The Friendship of Hamlin Garland and W. D. Howells". Papers on Language and Literature, 2006, 42(3): 264-290.

② Pritchard W H. "Howells and the Right American Stuff". The Hudson Review, 2011, 63(4): 549-570.

true nature. He engages these questions most directly in verse written in what author William Dean Howells described as literary English.[1]

9. Ethical Study

D. M. Yeager, in "'Art for Huamnity's Sake': The Social Novel as a Mode of Moral Discourse", argues that the social novel ought not to be confused with didacticism in literature and ought not to be expected to provide prescriptions for the cure of social ills. Neither should it necessarily be viewed as ephemeral. After examining justifications of the social novel offered by William Dean Howells (in the 1880s) and Jonathan Franzen (in the 1990s), the author explores the way in which social novels alter perceptions and responses at levels of sensibility that are not usually susceptible to rational argument, push back moral horizons, contribute to the creation of social conscience, and expose the complexity and contextuality of moral discernment. As a concrete example, Howells's 1889 novel *A Hazard of New Fortunes* is analyzed (and defended against its detractors) in terms of its sophisticated treatment of the dilemmas that arise from a recognition of personal complicity in structural sin, its disclosure of the context-indexed evolution of values, and its attention to the importance and fragility of social trust.[2]

---

[1] Smethurst J E. "Paul Laurence Dunbar and Turn-into-the-20th-Century African American Dualism". African American Review, 2007, 41(2): 377-386.

[2] Yeager D M. "'Art for Huamnity's Sake': The Social Novel as a Mode of Moral Discourse". Journal of Religious Ethics, 2005, 33(3): 445-485.

Chapter 7

Henry James

Henry James (1843-1916)

His dedication to literature for fifty years from the Civil War until his death in 1916 produced a body of work of monumental scope. He never married, never carried on anything resembling a conventional courtship. His friendships were virtually all rooted in shared literary or artistic enthusiasm. He travelled often, it seems, merely to reinvigorate himself for a new assault upon his artistic problems. With less talent and similar dedication, he might have produced novels and tales that consisted mainly of the same stories retold, the same techniques exploited again and again in order to recapture prior successes. Something of this tendency resides in his work as it does in the work of all masters, but there is also an extraordinary continual development that reaches its peak in these late masterpieces: *The Wings of the Dove*, *The Ambassadors*, and *The Golden Bowl*. The late work of some poets can best be read largely in the light of the education gained by studying their earlier efforts. James is one of a relatively few novelists whose work cries out to be approaches in a similar manner.

Critical Perspectives

1. Thematic Study

Elsa Nettels, in "Willa Cather and the Example of Henry James", offers information on American author Henry James, who influenced author Willa Cather in her initial days of her career. Topics discussed include Cather's first novel *Alexander's Bridge*, themes and techniques developed by James and Cather to engage the imagination of the reader and invite their participation in the text, and documents that contain Cather's early knowledge and admiration of James.[①]

Geoffrey R. Kirsch, in "Henry James, Inheritance, and the Problem of the Dead Hand", addresses how American fiction writer Henry James wrestled with the dead hand dilemma in many of his literary works and analyzes how the concept came to exist not only in American law, but also in American culture. James's life entangled with the problem of the dead hand on many occasions, which likely explains his fascination with the topic. John Chipman Gray, James's friend, became one of Harvard's most memorable law professors when he published his treatise *The Rule against Perpetuities*, which contained the seemingly simplistic formulation of the rule, which law students continue to learn. Years earlier, James's father contested the will of James's grandfather and prevailed when the court ruled that the grandfather's conditions violated *The Rule against Perpetuities*. Although James Sr. overcame the oppressive dead hand imposed by his father, his

---

① Nettels E. "Willa Cather and the Example of Henry James". Cather Studies, 2015(10): 189-222.

father's behavior exemplifies traditional principles of trust and estate law in the United States. *The Uniform Trust Code* supports the notion that no child has a right to inherit, and therefore, courts may not terminate trusts when termination would disturb a material purpose of the trust. A bizarre condition to inheritance may constitute a material purpose and, under traditional doctrine, courts should not disturb such conditions. Conversely, James Jr. likely would approve of the Restatement (Third) of Trusts, which allows modification when the reasons for modification outweigh the material purpose. ①

Sara Lyons, in " ' You Must Be as Clever as We Think You ' : Assessing Intelligence in Henry James's *The Tragic Muse*", explores how intelligence is represented in the works of Henry James, a writer who is regarded as one of the key figures of 19th-century literary realism. Presented are a discussion on the epistemological drama staged by the late fiction of James, an analysis of the characters in James' novel *The Spoils of Poynton*, and an examination of the nineteenth-century genealogy of the concept of intelligence quotient(IQ). ②

2. New-historicism

Stephen Miller, in "Henry James & the Great War", features author Henry James and his experiences in World War Ⅰ. Other topics include James' friendship with historian Henry Adams, how the war prevented James from writing his books *A Sense of the Past* and *The Ivory Tower*, James' contributions to the war including his leadership position in the group American Volunteer Motor Ambulance Corps, and

---

① Kirsch G R. "Henry James, Inheritance, and the Problem of the Dead Hand". Real Property, Trust and Estate Law Journal, 2013, 47(3): 435-465.

② Lyons S. " ' You Must Be as Clever as We Think You ' : Assessing Intelligence in Henry James's *The Tragic Muse*". Modern Philology, 2017, 115(1): 105-130.

his relationships with politicians like Winston Churchill and Ian Hamilton.①

Jennifer McDonell, in "Henry James, Literary Fame, and the Problem of Robert Browning", examines Robert Browning's and Henry James's writings to consider their responses to, and implication in the production, circulation, and consumption of late nineteenth-century celebrity. For James, there were two Brownings—the private, unknowable genius and the social personality. From the time he first met Browning until 1912, James held to this theory in letters, essays, biography, and fiction; the Browning "problem" became integral to James's fascinated engagement with other problems at the heart of celebrity culture. Both writers attacked celebrity discourses and practices (biography, interviews and literary tourism) that constructed the life as a vital source of meaning, threatening to displace the writers' work as privileged object of literary interpretation. Browning preceded James in insisting that the separation of public and private life was foundational to an impersonal aesthetics, and in exploring the fatal confusion between art and life that has been identified by theorists as central to celebrity culture.②

Leo Robson, in "The Master's Servants: On Henry James", discusses the history of the critical reception of author Henry James, focusing on 2012 conferences titled "A Stray Savage in Oxford: A Henry James Centenary Symposium" and "Placing Henry James" in England, and the book *Monopolizing the Master: Henry James and the Politics of Modern Literary Scholarship* by Michael Anesko. Literary scholars such as Christopher Ricks, Philip Horne, and Leon Edel are discussed, as well as poetic elements in James' work.③

---

① Miller S. "Henry James & the Great War". The New Criterion, 2022, 40(6): 33-35.
② McDonell J. "Henry James, Literary Fame, and the Problem of Robert Browning". Critical Survey, 2015, 27(3): 43-62.
③ Robson L. "The Master's Servants: On Henry James". The Nation, 2012, 295(20): 27-34.

Peter Collister, in "Shakespeare for Tourists: Henry James's *The Birthplace*", presents a literary criticism of the short story *The Birthplace* by Henry James. It outlines the characters and explores their symbolic significance. It examines the enactment of the story in a certain location and the references to the aspects of the tourism industry, including the late Victorian debate on national heritage, the development and preservation of sites of historic interest, and the dangers and pressures of commercialism. [1]

3. Psychoanalytical Study

Barbara Young, in "*The Beast in the Jungle*: Henry James 1843-1916", focuses on author Henry James, and his book *The Beast in the Jungle*. In this book, James tells the story of John Marcher, a man who was not able to turn the tables on his ghost. According to the author, Henry James, just like the character in his book, was a neurotic cripple from early childhood, and was aware of being so. The article speculates both on the sources of James's neurosis and on his remarkable resilience in overcoming adversity and making the most of what he had. [2]

Barbara Young, in "'The Great Good Place' Where the Great Want Is Met: Psychoanalytic Reflections on the Short Story by Henry James", argues that Henry James was a prolific storyteller who supported himself by his writing. During times of frustration and disappointment, he would become depressed. His therapy was to keep busy with his pen. Though much of his writing is difficult to read, his astute observations of people's psychological functioning make the reading all worthwhile.

---

[1] Collister P. "Shakespeare for Tourists: Henry James's *The Birthplace*". Modern Philology, 2019, 116(4): 377-400.

[2] Young B. "*The Beast in the Jungle*: Henry James 1843-1916". International Journal of Applied Psychoanalytic Studies, 2008, 5(4): 225-237.

In his later years, beginning with this story, he became more self-observant, and his stories increasingly draw on his own childhood emotional experiences and become cautionary tales about how best to live one's life. This story precedes *The Beast in the Jungle* by five years.①

Matthew Schilleman, in "Typewriter Psyche: Henry James's Mechanical Mind", shows that the mental model found in Henry James's late works derives from his switch to typewritten dictation. While dictating to the typewriter, James says that words are effectively and unceasingly "pulled out" of him by what he calls the "music" of the machine. The "click" of the Remington actually acts as a "positive spur" to his speech, resulting in a diffuseness that makes keeping any text within the length specified by the publisher virtually impossible for him. Critics have left these material effects of the writing machine largely unexamined. But through careful investigation, it can be demonstrated that the properties of typewritten dictation play a crucial role in forming the dynamic system of drives, compulsions, repetitions, and displacements for which James's late works are famous.②

4. Marxism Study

Paraic Finnerty, in "'Celebrities of the Future': Fame and Notability in Henry James's *Roderick Hudson* and *The American*", examines Henry James's deployment of imagery of statuary, performance, and display to foreground conflicts between emergent forms of notability and older ideas of aristocratic renown, and his use of the figure of the American in Europe to draw attention to the complex

---

① Young B. "'The Great Good Place' Where the Great Want Is Met: Psychoanalytic Reflections on the Short Story by Henry James". International Journal of Applied Psychoanalytic Studies, 2009, 6 (1): 84-92.

② Schilleman M. "Typewriter Psyche: Henry James's Mechanical Mind". Journal of Modern Literature, 2013, 36(3): 14-30.

intersections of nationality and gender in constructions of public recognition. *Roderick Hudson* positions the eponymous American sculptor as a lion in Europe, but reveals his fatal attempts to transcend the objectification and commodification accompanying fame. In *The American* (1877), Christopher Newman is briefly lionized by a French aristocratic family, but afterwards publicly spurned. Both novels contrast the fate of American men with the successful use of mechanisms of fame by women. *Roderick Hudson*'s Christina Light successfully markets her beauty, through her marriage to a figure of aristocratic renown, while *The American*'s Noémie Nioche negotiates her rise in the world through self-promotion, finally passing as a noblewoman. ①

5. Narrative Study

Lindsay Munnelly, in "Obstinate Objects: Agency as Immobility in Henry James's *The Spoils of Poynton*", reconsiders the representation of "things" in Henry James's fiction with a reading of his novel *The Spoils of Poynton*. The aristocratic characters employ various hermeneutics to interpret and thus claim the titular spoils, the things themselves exert agency by withdrawing from these interpretations. Using Graham Harman's object-oriented realism, entities must be understood independently of their relations to humans. ②

Daniel P. Gunn, in "Reading Strether: Authorial Narration and Free Indirect Discourse in *The Ambassadors*", argues that in part because of Henry James's own emphasis on the "rigour" of his practice, the strict limitation of *The Ambassadors* to

---

① Finnerty P. "'Celebrities of the Future': Fame and Notability in Henry James's *Roderick Hudson* and *The American*". Critical Survey, 2015, 27(3): 24-42.

② Munnelly L. "Obstinate Objects: Agency as Immobility in Henry James's *The Spoils of Poynton*". Texas Studies in Literature and Language, 2019, 61(1): 72-93.

Strether's point of view has dominated critical discussions of the novel's narrative technique. This essay argues that authorial narration plays a more prominent role in *The Ambassadors* than has previously been recognized and that the narrator's efforts to read and describe Strether's consciousness parallel Strether's own interpretive activity. Even during instances of free indirect discourse (FID), the narrator of *The Ambassadors* is a consistent presence, describing Strether's consciousness in precise, evocative detail and modeling for the reader a posture of careful and responsive attention to otherness. In this respect, the essay's argument about narration bears on one of the central conceptual questions in the theory of FID—that is, whether the two subjectivities (narratorial and figural) evoked by FID coexist, with the figural subjectivity contained or framed by the subjectivity of the narrator—or whether, instead, narratorial subjectivity simply disappears in FID, replaced or superseded by figural subjectivity. Finally, *The Ambassadors* is a sustained exercise in reading—reading the subtle grammar of the Jamesian sentence, reading delicate shifts in subjectivity or reference, and reading the suggestions and intonations in dialogue—and its subject matter is Strether's reading of the characters around him and his own cognition and perception. The novel's narrative technique mirrors this preoccupation with reading—and with the ethical implications of reading—by incorporating the perspective of an attentive external reader or observer into the text, in the presence of the narrator.[①]

6. Post-colonial Study

Irem Balkir, in "Henry James and the 'Imperial Feeling'", alludes to an imperial feeling in the works of Henry James during the mid-1880's. Topics

---

① Gunn D P. "Reading Strether: Authorial Narration and Free Indirect Discourse in *The Ambassadors*". Narrative, 2017, 25(1): 28-44.

discussed include imperialism as the harbinger of cultural corruption; ethical disaffection with power desires; politicization of James' critical language; opposition to expansionism despite affirmation of its moralizing legitimacy; and interpretations of cosmopolitanism unmarred by race-ideological discourses. [1]

7. Religious Study

Kyriaki Asiatiodu, in "*The Turn of the Screw* and *Daisy Miller*: Henry James's Puritan View on the Ideal Victorian Middle-class", sheds light upon a nineteenth-century reader-response approach to *The Turn of the Screw* and *Daisy Miller*, grounded on an ethical basis that is shaped by dominant Victorian values, beliefs, and ideas concerning the catalytic role of family towards the proper raising of children, the importance of duty, the traits of the ideal woman and mother, and the good or evil nature of people who are members of different socioeconomic classes, all of which are controlling factors of (un)restrained sexuality and its impact on social order. Within this context, the writer of this article claims that in both stories, Henry James is interested in pointing out the threat of a general moral corruption that characterizes the Western world of his time, particularly the socio-economically powerful nineteenth-century Anglo-Saxon middle-class, with the latter vacillating between excessive freedom/naivity and excessive rigidness/ hypocricy. Furthermore, the writer claims the complementary character of the two stories. Although *Daisy Miller* chronologically preceeds *The Turn of the Screw*, the latter's examination prior to a discussion of *Daisy Miller* may be helpful because *The Turn of the Screw* is a more complete work in the sense that elaborates more on the moral and psychological condition of characters who strikingly resemble those in the story of

---

[1] Balkir I. "Henry James and the 'Imperial Feeling'". American Studies International, 1995, 33 (2): 17-31.

Daisy Miller.①

Bryan Berry, in "Henry James and the Heavenly Light", discusses the themes of communal worship and the cultural importance of churches in works by Henry James. The theme of spiritual connection is evident in his novel *The Golden Bowl*. The article compares James' works to that of Nathaniel Hawthorne, where Hawthorne's writings contain similar themes of upholding social conventions in the face of evil. It also comments on James' visit to the United States in 1904, where he wrote about the visible absence of churches.②

8. Biological Study

Edward Short, in "Henry James and the Ties of Family", discusses works of Henry James, and explores his progressive ideology. It mentions that James had imbibed as a boy in New York and in its psychological acuity, which exemplifies obviously in his finest fiction. It discusses that peculiar drama of consciousness depicted in the writings of James.③

J. Russell Perkin, in "Imagining Henry: Henry James as a Fictional Character in Colm Tóibín's *The Master* and David Lodge's *Author, Author*", explores the hybrid genre of the "biographical novel" through a comparison of Colm Tóibín's *The Master* and David Lodge's *Author, Author*. There are some striking similarities between these two works, and this reveals the extent to which Henry James's version of his own life has given shape to all subsequent accounts of it. At the same

---

① Asiatiodu K. "*The Turn of the Screw* and *Daisy Miller*: Henry James's Puritan View on the Ideal Victorian Middle-class". Gaziantep University Journal of Social Sciences, 2018, 17(3): 820-833.

② Berry B. "Henry James and the Heavenly Light". First Things: A Monthly Journal of Religion & Public Life, 2006(167): 34-37.

③ Short E. "Henry James and the Ties of Family". The Human Life Review, 2022, 48(2): 44-47.

time, each novelist gives us a Henry James in his own image, and Harold Bloom's theory of literary history helps us to understand how Lodge and Tóibín have attempted to overcome the influence of a writer that each of them holds in very high regard.①

Lee Clark Mitchell, in "'Dawdling and Gaping': James's *A Small Boy and Others*", argues that *A Small Boy and Others* is rarely discussed for failing to explain the artist Henry James—indeed, for failing to cohere as narrative at all. The reason for both of these failures is due in part to James's two-dimensional depiction of himself as a youth, "wondering and dawdling and gaping", and in part to the nature of the narrator who mirrors that earlier self, also lost in wonder. This symbiosis of "small boy" and aged artist subverts an autobiographical logic by lauding both earlier and present selves as passive receptacles. The question is why James deliberately mystifies readers this way, given the care with which he reconstructed his past. The answer is that his personal reasons for revisiting his past coincided with a set of different assumptions about consciousness and psychology that had informed his late novels.②

9. Philosophical Study

Roger Duncan, in "William and Henry James on the Immortality of the Soul", offers the insights of American philosophers and authors William James and Henry James regarding the immorality of the human soul. William James concludes that human thought expresses the function of brain activity, and Henry James also added

---

① Perkin J R. "Imagining Henry: Henry James as a Fictional Character in Colm Tóibín's *The Master* and David Lodge's *Author, Author*". Journal of Modern Literature, 2010, 33(2): 114-130.

② Mitchell L C. "'Dawdling and Gaping': James's *A Small Boy and Others*". Journal of Modern Literature, 2015, 39(1): 1-18.

that the hypothesis of material realm is a serviceable and thin veil for the breakthrough of consciousness.①

Peter Collister, in "Henry James, the 'Scenic Idea', and *Nona Vincent*", focuses on short story *Nona Vincent* by Henry James, and James's idea of the scene and the making of a scene. It states that existing theme of James's life narrative entails the development of artistic sensibility and despite mixed dramatic and emotional rewards, Henry continued to offer devotions to dramatic form. It mentions that James's private theatricals and improvised figurative drama of scenes making executed represent emblems and form part of social and ritualistic continuum of events.②

10. Ethical Study

Christopher J. Stuart, in "Ethics and Evidence: Authorial Intention and Sedgwick's 'Reading Marcher Straight'", focuses on the critical principles Henry James outlines in *The Art of Fiction* against the post-structuralist interpretive procedures, which Eve Kosofsky Sedgwick employs in her interpretation of James's own story *The Beast in the Jungle*. In order to reveal the significant ethical and evidentiary costs of a criticism, this essay treats the demonstration of authorial intent as a luxury rather than as a standard of responsible literary interpretation.③

---

① Duncan R. "William and Henry James on the Immortality of the Soul". Logos: A Journal of Catholic Thought and Culture, 2015, 18(2): 175-188.
② Collister P. "Henry James, the 'Scenic Idea', and *Nona Vincent*". Philological Quarterly 2015, 94(3): 267-290.
③ Stuart C J. "Ethics and Evidence: Authorial Intention and Sedgwick's 'Reading Marcher Straight'". Texas Studies in Literature and Language, 2019(61): 1-27.

11. Cultural Study

Hossein Nazari and Parisa Pooyandeh, in "From the American Eve to the European(ized) Eve in Henry James's *The Portrait of a Lady*", explore the concept of the American Eve to the Europeanized Eve in Henry James' novel *The Portrait of a Lady*. Topics discussed are development process of the protagonist Isabel Archer which reinforced her psychological and intellectual transformation through social encounter with American and European cultures, Isabel's theory of marriage and idea of happiness, cultural conflict between American and European lifestyles and values, gender role and social expectations on women. [①]

Shawna Ross, in "'This Wild Hunt for Rest': Working at Play in *The Ambassadors*", argues that both scholarship on the literature of travel and emergent theories of the transnational have ignored the key roles played by twentieth-century philosophies and institutions of leisure. This article begins to consider the cultural and material history of leisure as a significant trope in modernism by identifying an aesthetics of leisure developed in Henry James's letters and fiction, particularly his late novel *The Ambassadors* (1903). The critical charge of this novel resides in its transformation of two contemporaneous discourses—the Protestant work ethic and its lesser-known but equally pervasive counterpart, the ideology of modern leisure—into an aesthetically productive dialectic of labor and leisure. Considering James's aesthetics of leisure as theme and style in his fiction and as a self-consciously elaborated mode of literary production in his non-fiction suggests the broader

---

① Nazari H, Pooyandeh P. "From the American Eve to the European(ized) Eve in Henry James's *The Portrait of a Lady*". Women's Studies, 2022, 51(3): 343-356.

significance of leisure for modernism.①

Jonathan Freedman, in "*The Ambassadors* and the Culture of Optical Illusion", presents on the intersections between visual perception and optical illusions, changes in media culture in the late 19th- and early 20th-centuries associated with the advent of motion pictures and related technologies, and the work of novelist Henry James, particularly the novel *The Ambassadors*. Topics include the pragmatist philosophical tradition, the work of psychology scholars William James and Joseph Jastrow, and philosopher Ludwig Wittgenstein, and unconscious mental processes.②

12. Feminism Study

Alfred Habegger, in "*The Bostonians* and Henry James Sr.'s Crusade against Feminism and Free Love", deals with the book *The Bostonians*, by Henry James. Topics discussed include realistic representation of the way the political infects the personal in American life; Pauline Kael's review of the motion picture version of the novel; need for all men to follow a long and painful process of self-correction; Henry James Sr.'s views on sex, love, and marriage; and struggle against nineteenth-century feminism and free love.③

Priscilla L. Walton, in "Down the Rabbit Hole: *The Bostonians* and Alice James", uses the life of Alice James to reread her brother Henry's novel, *The Bostonians*. Alice, who was a partner in a Boston marriage, and her illnesses, of

---

① Ross S. "'This Wild Hunt for Rest': Working at Play in *The Ambassadors*". Journal of Modern Literature, 2013, 37(1): 1-20.

② Freedman J. "*The Ambassadors* and the Culture of Optical Illusion". Raritan, 2015, 34(3): 133-157.

③ Habegger A. "*The Bostonians* and Henry James Sr.'s Crusade against Feminism and Free Love". Women's Studies, 1988, 15(4): 323-342.

which she wrote in her letters and diary, provide a means of reassessing the gender dynamics of James's only novel about suffrage and the women's movement. Her life sheds light on and offers an alternative reading of the novel's problematic heteronormative movement. ①

13. Comparative Study

Buse Eren, in "Henry James's *The Portrait of a Lady* (1881) or Jane Campion's 1996 Movie Adaptation?", aims at identifying both the similarities and differences between Henry James's novel *The Portrait of a Lady* (1881) and Jane Campion's 1996 movie version. This essay tries to answer the following questions. Is a Modernist literary piece still appealing to the 21st century readers? What is lost and what is gained from the screen adaptation of the book? Would a person reading the novel be interested in watching the movie and vice versa? Last but not least, the essay compares the portrayal of the characters in the novel and their materialization in the movie through the parts of Nicole Kidman, John Malkovich, Barbara Hershey and Mary-Louise Parker. ②

---

① Walton P L. "Down the Rabbit Hole: *The Bostonians* and Alice James". Canadian Review of American Studies, 2015, 45(1): 67-82.

② Eren B. "Henry James's *The Portrait of a Lady* (1881) or Jane Campion's 1996 Movie Adaptation?" Journal of History, Culture and Art Research, 2015, 4(3): 1-7.

Chapter 8

Mark Twain

Mark Twain (1835-1910)

Samuel Langhorne Clemens, better known as Mark Twain, remains one of America's most widely read authors. To a great extent, his popularity has rested upon his humor. It would be a mistake, however, to think of him simply as a humorist. To do so is to overlook the sharpness of his observation, the penetration of his social criticism, the depth of his concern for human suffering, and the charity and extraordinary beauty of his style. Much that Twain wrote was topical and overwrought, and it slides into oblivion. But his best works remain unrivalled in their depiction of the comic and the pathetic in life. William Dean Howells, Twains' best friend for forty years, composed a fitting epitaph when he wrote that Mark Twain was "sole, incomparable, the Lincoln of our literature". [1]

---

[1] https://www.britannica.com/biography/Mark-Twain/Reputation-and-legacy.

Critical Perspectives

1. Thematic Study

Jarret S. Lovell, in "On Field Mice, Butterflies, and Tigers: Mark Twain's *Ten Commandments* and Circumstance-based Justice", offers insights regarding the essay of Mark Twain titled "Fables of Man", which focuses on the identities of two murderers. He mentions that Twain has used direct and clear language to illustrate criminal justice system. He argues that *The Ten Commandments* cannot alter the circumstance or temperament of animals while penal law can do less to tackle the economic, social and emotional circumstances of criminals.[1]

2. New-historicism

Stanley Finger, in "Mark Twain's Phrenological Experiment: Three Renditions of His 'Small Test'", argues that Samuel Langhorne Clemens, the American humorist and author better known as Mark Twain, is skeptical about clairvoyance, supernatural entities, palm reading, and certain medical fads, including phrenology. During the early 1870s, he set forth to test phrenology—and, more specifically, its reliance on craniology—by undergoing two head examinations with Lorenzo Fowler, an American phrenologist with an institute in London. Twain

---

[1] Lovell J S. "On Field Mice, Butterflies, and Tigers: Mark Twain's *Ten Commandments* and Circumstance-based Justice". Contemporary Justice Review, 2012, 15(2): 173-176.

hid his identity during his first visit, but not when he returned as a new customer three months later, only to receive a very different report about his humor, courage, and so on. He described his experiences in a short letter written in 1906 to a correspondent in London, in humorous detail in a chapter that appeared in a posthumous edition of his autobiography, and in *The Secret History of Eddypus, the World Empire*, a work of fiction involving time travel, which he began to write around 1901 but never completed. All three versions of Twain's phrenological ploy are presented here with commentary to put his descriptions in perspective. ①

Thomas Ruys Smith, in "Life on the Mississippi", discusses how author Mark Twain portrayed life on the Mississippi River in his writings. Topics explored include his childhood in Hannibal, Missouri, which allowed him to be exposed to transportation and alleged slave trade operations through the river, the way he featured the river in his novels *The Adventures of Tom Sawyer* and *Adventures of Huckleberry Finn*, and the significant economic contributions of the river acknowledged by Twain. ②

Stanley Finger, in "Mark Twain's Life-long Fascination with Phrenology", argues that Samuel Langhorne Clemens (Mark Twain), American humorist and writer, followed scientific and medical developments, and relished exposing questionable practices and ideas. In his youth, he pondered how phrenologists were assessing character, and in 1855 he copied sections of a phrenology book and a skull diagram into a notebook. Later, in London, he had two phrenological examinations by Lorenzo Fowler—one without and the other after identifying himself. Following his "test", which produced contrasting results, he began to ridicule phrenologists and phrenology in *Tom Sawyer*, *Huckleberry Finn*, and other

---

① Finger S. "Mark Twain's Phrenological Experiment: Three Renditions of His 'Small Test'". Journal of the History of the Neurosciences, 2020, 29(1): 101-118.

② Smith T R. "Life on the Mississippi". History Today, 2019, 69(9): 42-53.

works. He underwent at least two more head readings in the United States, and in *Eddypus*, an unfinished work from 1901 to 1902, he maintained that phrenologists base their insights primarily on how people dress and answer questions. Although now lampooning the craniological tenets of phrenology, Twain never seemed to reject the idea of distinct faculties of mind associated with specialized brain organs. [①]

James E. Caron, in "Mark Twain Reports on Commerce with the Hawaiian Kingdom", talks about the role of author Samuel Clemens, who was usually published under the pseudonym Mark Twain, in reporting on U.S. commerce with the Kingdom of Hawai'i. According to the author, Clemens used his popular literary persona to promote capitalist investment in the country. It is suggested that his enthusiasm for possible commercial successes in Hawai'i overrode his political and journalistic instincts. Particular focus is given to the role of steamships in his reportage. [②]

Mark Storey, in "Huck and Hank Go to the Circus: Mark Twain under Barnum's Big Top", argues that Mark Twain's acquaintance with P. T. Barnum, and more especially Twain's fascination with the world of popular entertainment that Barnum epitomized, provided inspiration and material for some of Twain's most enduring works. In particular, the essay argues that two of Twain's most revered novels—*The Adventures of Huckleberry Finn* (1884) and *A Connecticut Yankee at King Arthur's Court* (1889)—are invested both thematically and generically in the complex cultural associations of the postbellum circus. Embodying the commercial capitalism of industrialized America whilst also offering a romantic liberation from everyday life, the circus becomes a condensation of many of the competing impulses of Twain's life and work—between irreverent humour and

---

① Finger S. "Mark Twain's Life-long Fascination with Phrenology". Journal of the History of the Behavioral Sciences, 2019, 55(2): 99-121.

② Caron J E. "Mark Twain Reports on Commerce with the Hawaiian Kingdom". The Hawaiian Journal of History, 2010(44): 37-56.

sober social critique, and between the desire for imaginative freedom and a recognition of financial imperatives. ①

3. Psychoanalytical Study

Steve Clarke, in "Huckleberry Finn's Conscience: Reckoning with the Evasion", argues that Huck Finn's struggles with his conscience, as depicted in Mark Twain's famous novel *The Adventures of Huckleberry Finn* (*AHF*) (1884), have been much discussed by philosophers. And various philosophical lessons have been extracted from Twain's depiction of those struggles. Two of these philosophers stand out, in terms of influence: Jonathan Bennett and Nomy Arpaly. Here the author of this essay argues that the lessons that Bennett and Arpaly draw are not supported by a careful reading of *AHF*. This becomes particularly apparent when readers consider the final part of the book, commonly referred to, by literary scholars, as "the evasion". During the evasion, Huck behaves in ways that are extremely difficult to reconcile with the interpretations of *AHF* offered by Bennett and Arpaly. This essay extracts a different philosophical lesson from *AHF* than either Bennett or Arpaly, which makes sense of the presence of the evasion in *AHF*. This lesson concerns the importance of conscious moral deliberation for moral guidance and for overcoming wrongful moral assumptions. This essay relies on an interpretation of *AHF* that is influential in literary scholarship. On it the evasion is understood as an allegory about US race relations during the 20-year period from the end of the US Civil War to the publication of *AHF*. ②

---

① Storey M. "Huck and Hank Go to the Circus: Mark Twain under Barnum's Big Top". European Journal of American Culture, 2010, 29(3): 217-228.

② Clarke S. "Huckleberry Finn's Conscience: Reckoning with the Evasion". The Journal of Ethics, 2020, 24(4): 485-508.

4. Marxism Study

Janko Trupej, in "A Comparison of the Pre-Socialist and Socialist Reception of Mark Twain in Slovenia", analyses the reception of Mark Twain and his works in serial publications on the territory that now constitutes the Republic of Slovenia over a period of circa one hundred years. It compares Twain's status in the pre-socialist era (until 1945) and the socialist era (1945-1991). The article addresses the extent to which the reception was affected by ideology and the contemporary political situation, as well as by the relations between the United States and the country of which the Slovenian territory formed part during a particular period of time.[①]

Scott Moore, in "The Code Duello and the Reified Self in Mark Twain's *Pudd'nhead Wilson*", examines the effect of regional attitudes on antebellum class structures depicted in Mark Twain's *Pudd'nhead Wilson*. The article notes that the southern code of honor, a dominating cultural force in the community Twain creates, mandates the duel as a way to defend and preserve one's honor and maintain one's standing among the social elite. It discusses how social class in the village is inherited, much as it was by the European aristocracy that drove many of these citizens' ancestors to seek freedom in the New World.[②]

5. Post-colonial Study

Kathleen Schultheis, in "Banning Huck: Why Mark Twain's *The Adventures*

[①] Trupej J. "A Comparison of the Pre-Socialist and Socialist Reception of Mark Twain in Slovenia". Annals for Istrian and Mediterranean Studies, 2021, 31(2): 295-310.

[②] Moore S. "The Code Duello and the Reified Self in Mark Twain's *Pudd'nhead Wilson*". American Transcendental Quarterly, 2008, 22(3): 499-515.

of Huckleberry Finn Belongs in English Literature Curriculum despite—Indeed Because of—Its Use of the N-Word", presents a literary criticism of the book *The Adventures of Huckleberry Finn* by Mark Twain. Topics include reports that it tells about the human spirit over slavery and its entanglement with every institution of American life, and examinations that he use an incendiary word in full knowledge of its ability to offend white America in the 19th century.[①]

Sally Riad and Gavin Jack, in "Tracing the Sphinx from Symbol to Specters: Reflections on the Organization of Geographies of Concern", argue that the concept of the gaze plays an important role in (post) colonial organizational analysis. It addresses dynamics of looking and being seen, particularly as they pertain to knowledge and identity. Drawing on Derrida's writing on spectrality as it intersects with text and aesthetics, critics can chart a theoretical framework with which they broaden and deepen extant approaches to the gaze. This essay illustrates its organizational dynamics across two vignettes that examine writing on the Sphinx by Hegel and Mark Twain. This essay also broadens the literature on the gaze with a new view on the (re)production of presence and absence. It also deepens reflection by outlining how the occupation of concern is shaped by interested blindness and unease at a gaze from a specter. These insights invite reconsideration of extant views on knowledge and identity within (post) colonial organizational analysis, and inspire reflection on how scholars can participate in tracing the organization of geographies of concern.[②]

---

① Schultheis K. "Banning Huck: Why Mark Twain's *The Adventures of Huckleberry Finn* Belongs in English Literature Curriculum despite—Indeed Because of—Its Use of the N-Word". Skeptic, 2021, 26(1): 46-49.

② Riad S, Jack G. "Tracing the Sphinx from Symbol to Specters: Reflections on the Organization of Geographies of Concern". Culture and Organization, 2021, 27(3): 240-266.

6. Biological Study

Yasuhiro Takeuchi, in "A Fascination with Corpses: Mark Twain's 'Shameful Behavior'", argues that throughout his career, Mark Twain exhibited both a fascination with and abhorrence of corpses. Time after time he returned to the subject as both the object of humor and of reflection. Very likely it began on 24 March 1847, when he saw the autopsy of his father's body through a keyhole. John M. Clemens, Twain's father, was caught in a sleet storm on 11 March 1847, and died of pneumonia within two weeks. Twain's feelings of horror seem to have a dominant influence throughout his personal life, since he never dared to refer to the incident directly even in his private notes. However, in his fiction writings, as if to find an outlet for the deep suppression of his traumatic experience, he is almost obsessed with corpses. [1]

James E. Caron, in "The Satirist Who Clowns: Mark Twain's Performance at the Whittier Birthday Celebration", discusses the performance of satire by Sam Clemens as well as Mark Twain's speech during the celebration of John Greenleaf Whittier's 70th birthday. It states that the event provided a historical narrative rationale and presented a tangle of motivations for the principal actors in the drama to literary critics and historians. It suggests that the use by Mark Twain of the concept Citizen Clown drew attention to the role of the satirist in 19th century American culture, which meant to reaffirm the holy sanctuary of highbrow literary aesthetics. [2]

---

[1] Takeuchi Y. "A Fascination with Corpses: Mark Twain's 'Shameful Behavior'". The Midwest Quarterly, 2013, 54(2): 202-217.

[2] Caron J E. "The Satirist Who Clowns: Mark Twain's Performance at the Whittier Birthday Celebration". Texas Studies in Literature and Language, 2010, 52(4): 433-466.

Regina Faden, in "Changing Old Institutions: Race in the Mark Twain Museum", discusses the developments of Mark Twain Boyhood Home and Museum in Hannibal, Missouri. The author notes that the changes at the museum was initiated in 2004, which comprised of an overarching theme of storytelling that would bind the museums properties, Twain's biography with the stories and characters inspired by his experience. It also states that its board has agreed to set an exhibit about the novel *The Adventures of Huckleberry Finn*. ①

7. Philosophical Study

Bennett Kravitz, in "Mark Twain's Satanic Existentialist: *The Mysterious Stranger*", attempts to situate Mark Twain's *The Mysterious Stranger* in the context of American optimism at the onset of the twentieth century. While often considered one of the most pessimistic of Twain's novels, *The Mysterious Stranger* is portrayed as Twain's engagement with the philosophy of existentialism. Specifically, the article examines the ways that the text engages the existential premises of Jean Paul Sartre. Rather than abandoning his American optimism, Twain essentially destroys the visible world of endless warfare and religious obstruction to allow Americans to reclaim their Emersonian optimism by suggesting that we all "Dream other dreams and better". This article argues that the margins of the text suggest an existential attempt to come to terms with the disappointments of the Gilded Age and the inconsistencies of early twentieth-century America and its capitalistic society. ②

---

① Faden R. "Changing Old Institutions: Race in the Mark Twain Museum". Arkansas Review: A Journal of Delta Studies, 2009, 40(1): 5-17.
② Kravitz B. "Mark Twain's Satanic Existentialist: *The Mysterious Stranger*". European Journal of American Culture, 2014, 33(1): 61-74.

8. Cultural Study

Todd Goddard, in "Mark Twain's Geographic Imagination in *Life on the Mississippi*", argues that Twain's relationship to and understanding of place is characterized by robust sense of nostalgic identification and attachment. Yet Twain demonstrates in *Life on the Mississippi* that place is inherently open and always in process. For Twain, place is more event than static object, more verb than noun. Rather than fixed and unchanging, it is an articulated moment in an ongoing and neverending process of change (both social and "natural") and a constant reordering of a constellation of social relations. Through an investigation of *Life on the Mississippi*, this paper explores Twain's articulation of a nostalgic and portable sense of place that ultimately resists what he sees as the inherent instability and inevitable dissolution of place. In doing so, Twain anticipates geographers like Doreen Massey by recognizing the radical openness and constant changeability of place. Indeed, by detailing the physical and cultural history of the Mississippi river, and through his elaborate description of his education as a riverboat pilot, Twain suggests that place itself can be preserved only in memory and only by those properly trained to read it. In addition, the paper explores recent critical debates on the nature of space and place, the relationship between temporality and spatiality, human interactions with landscape and environment, as well as the tensions between the local and the global. [1]

Kerry Driscoll, in "Pearls from the Archive", focuses on archives at the Connecticut Historical Society, trying to learn more about author Mark Twain's

---

[1] Goddard T. "Mark Twain's Geographic Imagination in *Life on the Mississippi*". Journal of the Utah Academy of Sciences, Arts & Letters, 2018(95): 185-202.

involvement with the Saturday Morning Club, an organization founded in 1876. It mentions that scrapbooks, unpaginated volumes arranged neither by chronology nor topic, are so crammed with random stuff-newspaper clippings, theater programs, personal correspondence, and ticket stub.①

---

① Driscoll K. "Pearls from the Archive". Mark Twain Circular, 2019, 33(1): 19-22.

Chapter 9

Theodore Dreiser

Theodore Dreiser (1871-1945)

Theodore Dreiser almost single-handedly creates and makes respectable a socially oriented fiction that surprisingly complements the romance tradition of Hawthorne and Melville, while expanding the narrowly focused realism of Howells and James. His achievement is vast, paradoxical, and considering the conditions of his birth and the poverty of his youth, highly unlikely. Personally ungainly, erratically educated, and processing an unusually shoddy conception of aesthetics, he succeeds through a combination of passionate integrity and a brutal determination to exhaust his material completely. For the first time in American fiction he introduced on an epic scale a literary effort in which the social environment was given a detailed attention equal to, if not greater than, that which was focused on the individual protagonist. His hires are neither orphans set adrift in a bewildering static world, nor are they archetypal symbols occupying spaced in a moral or categorical diagram. Instead they are begotten out of concrete family relationships within particular socio-economic situation. And although Dreiser's characters are never the mere pawns of their social and biological circumstances, still they can only be understood in terms of those circumstances. Sex and money have ever been the twin thematic strands out of which novels are built, but Dreiser is the first American novelist to scrutinize these concerns with a consistently unashamed and unaverred gaze.

Critical Perspectives

1. Thematic Study

Donna Packer-Kinlaw, in "Through 'the Rose Window of the West': Nostalgia, Gothicism, and the Imaginary in Theodore Dreiser's *A Hoosier Holiday*", examines American novelist, Theodore Dreiser's reasons for returning to his boyhood home in Indiana and the psychological pain he experienced upon re-entering that world. It highlights the complexity of nostalgia and the potential hazards. It also aims to shift the focus from Dreiser's relationship with modernity to understand how nostalgia distorted his memories. [1]

Donald Pizer, in "Otto Weiningeer and the Sexual Dynamics of Theodore Dreiser's *The 'Genius'*", presents a literary criticism of the novel *The "Genius"*, by Theodore Dreiser. It highlights the novel's fuzzy and self-indulgent themes and its unselective dramatization of the life of the protagonist as artist and lover. It explores the relationship of the novel with the 1906 treatise *Sex and Character*, by Otto Weininger. The representation of sexual desire in the character's life and art is analyzed. [2]

Roark Mulligan, in "Dreiser's Murder Ballad", covers the subject of murder ballads in fiction and real life. It reviews the masterpiece of Theodore Dreiser, *An*

---

[1] Packer-Kinlaw D. "Through 'the Rose Window of the West': Nostalgia, Gothicism, and the Imaginary in Theodore Dreiser's *A Hoosier Holiday*". Studies in American Naturalism, 2022, 17(1): 1-21.

[2] Pizer D. "Otto Weiningeer and the Sexual Dynamics of Theodore Dreiser's *The 'Genius'*". Studies in American Naturalism, 2011, 6(1): 120-130.

American Tragedy, a novel about young Clyde Griffiths murders the farmer's pregnant daughter, Roberta Alden. There is an analysis of the fictional murder ballad being inspired by real life murders, as in the murder of Grace Brown by Chester Gillette, and that of Pearl Bryan by Jackson and Alonzo in Kentucky. The essay includes an account of Dreiser's brother, Paul Dresser, who made his success as a musical composer.①

2. New-historicism

Kiyohiko Murayama, in "Lynching as an American Tragedy in Theodore Dreiser", explores writer Theodore Dreiser's idea of tragedy and its role in his development as a novelist. Topics discussed include the influence of lynchings of whites and African Americans in the U. S. from 1889 to 1932 in his novel *An American Tragedy* and in other fiction and journalistic works, the close link of race and sex in lynching, and lynching as a ritual process to restore community order. Also noted is Dreiser's hostility to the U. S. judicial system.②

Mark Schiebe, in "The Rembrandts of Investment: Collecting Art and Money in the *Trilogy of Desire*", presents a literary criticism of the book *Trilogy of Desire* by Theodore Dreiser. It outlines author's collection which grows to become one of the most impressive in the country and discusses about art collector Frank Cowperwood who would have been enthusiastic about owning a percentage of a Rembrandt. It also highlights that Cowperwood's collection, as a manifestation of his insatiable acquisitive drive, is analogous with his growing collection of

---

① Mulligan R. "Dreiser's Murder Ballad". Studies in American Naturalism, 2008, 3 (1): 22-41.
② Murayama K. "Lynching as an American Tragedy in Theodore Dreiser". Mississippi Quarterly, 2017/2018, 70/71(2): 163-180.

mistresses.[①]

Jennifer Travis, in "Injury's Accountant: Theodore Dreiser and the Railroad", discusses an aspect of the life of Theodore Dreiser, the U. S. writer and naturalist. It focuses on Dreiser's suffering as a railroad worker, mainly from his mental condition brought about by nervous anxiety due to neurasthenia. It was after his departure from the sanitarium of William Muldoon that Dreiser sought employment with the New York Central Railroad with expectations that the labor would help him in his writing. On the railroad, he puts his life, sufferings and psychological wounds into his unfinished work, *An Amateur Laborer*.[②]

3. Gender Study

Carol A. Nathanson, in "Anne Estelle Rice and *Ellen Adams Wrynn*: Dreiser's Perspectives on Gender and Gendered Perspectives on Art", focuses on the influence of Anne Estelle Rice, a modernist painter, on the perspectives of author Theodore Dreiser. This essay mainly talks about Theodore Dreiser's views on gender and gendered perspectives on art. Topics discussed include relationship of Rice with Dreiser; her presence in the literature written by Dreiser, entitled "Ellen Adams Wrynn"; and Dreiser's view on how the external feminine manifests itself in visual art.[③]

---

① Schiebe M. "The Rembrandts of Investment: Collecting Art and Money in the *Trilogy of Desire*". Studies in American Naturalism, 2018, 13(2): 165-181.

② Travis J. "Injury's Accountant: Theodore Dreiser and the Railroad". Studies in American Naturalism, 2008, 3(1): 42-59.

③ Nathanson C A. "Anne Estelle Rice and *Ellen Adams Wrynn*: Dreiser's Perspectives on Gender and Gendered Perspectives on Art". Dreiser Studies, 2001, 32(1): 3-35.

4. Narrative Study

Thomas P. Riggio, in "Oh Captain, My Captain: Dreiser and the Chaplain of Madison Square", focuses on an analysis of the Captain character in *Sister Carrie* by Theodore Dreiser. Topics discussed include consideration of critic Ellen Moers over the Captain as an independent character developed by Dreiser; representation of uniqueness towards a character by Dreiser in his literary creations; and illustration of naturalism representation in the book by Dreiser through the character.[①]

5. Religious Study

Nadjia Amrane, in "Theodore Dreiser's Relevance to the Modern Moslem World", discusses the relevance of Theodore Dreiser's writings in the modern Moslem world by giving the analysis of the Moslem world. There is some significance of Dreiser's novels to modern Moslem readers and it is through an assessment of Dreiser's popularity due to the attractive features of Dreiser's novels.[②]

6. Social Study

Annette R. Dolph, in "Contextualizing the Garden: The Ambiguity of Nature in Dreiser's *The Bulwark*", presents a literary criticism of the novel *The Bulwark*, by Theodore Dreiser. The novel presents the story of three generations of a Quaker

---

① Riggio T P. "Oh Captain, My Captain: Dreiser and the Chaplain of Madison Square". Studies in American Naturalism, 2016, 11(2): 23-37.
② Amrane N. "Theodore Dreiser's Relevance to the Modern Moslem World". Dreiser Studies, 2003, 34(2): 44-56.

family amid economic gain, modernization and social change. It chronicles the temptations of materialism that affected the children. The representation of a garden in the novel is discussed. The conflicts among family members are also analyzed. [1]

7. Ecological Study

Cara Elana Erdheim, in "Is There a Place for Ecology in *An American Tragedy*? Wealth, Water, and the Dreiserian Struggle for Survival", discusses various writings of U.S. writer and naturalist Theodore Dreiser. It presents his views and socio-political position on the relationship between the environment, ecology and social classes. In his 1925 masterpiece, *An American Tragedy*, he writes of the life and struggles of the young Clyde Griffiths amidst America's nobility. In the novel, there are allusions of injustice amongst social classes as to access to natural resources, such as water. Dreiser's other writings on the same theme are also reviewed. [2]

8. Biological Study

Kiyohiko Murayama, in "Theodore Dreiser and the Modernists", focuses on an assessment of writing approaches of writer Theodore Dreiser along with his association with modernists. Topics discussed include depiction of praise for Dreiser in an acceptance speech for Nobel Prize by Sinclair Lewis; observation of cultural transformation in society after the World War Ⅰ leads to distinction between prewar

---

[1] Dolph A R. "Contextualizing the Garden: The Ambiguity of Nature in Dreiser's *The Bulwark*". Studies in American Naturalism, 2011, 6(1): 103-119.

[2] Erdheim C E. "Is There a Place for Ecology in *An American Tragedy*? Wealth, Water, and the Dreiserian Struggle for Survival". Studies in American Naturalism, 2008, 3(1): 3-21.

and postwar writers; and comparison of Dreiser and author William Faulkner's writing despite of Faulkner's indebtness towards Dreiser.①

Roark Mulligan, in "Thomas P. Riggio on Theodore Dreiser Studies", discusses the studies on the works of author Theodore Dreiser by University of Connecticut English professor Thomas P. Riggio. Riggio recognizes the importance of Dreiser's biographies written by Burton Rascoe and Dorothy Dudley to *Dreiser Studies*. He believes that the letters written by Dreiser to various women have significance to his works. Riggio also addressed the influence of Dreiser to realists and modernists in one of his essays.②

Mandy See, in "'It Was Written That We Meet': The Collaborative Friendship of Theodore Dreiser and George Douglas", discusses the contributions of author George Douglas to the life and works of author Theodore Dreiser. Topics discussed include details of the friendship between Douglas and Dreiser; background of Douglas; and information on the Dreiser's book *Notes on Life*.③

Jack Dvorak, in "May Calvert: Dreiser's Lifelong Teacher", discusses the influence of teacher May Calvert on the formal education of novelist Theodore Dreiser and the attitude of Dreiser toward the public school environment when he was in seventh-grade in Warsaw, Poland. Topics discussed include the efforts of Calvert to help her student develop his grammar skills and writing and speaking ability.④

Roger W. Smith, in "A Dreiser Checklist, 2004", presents a bibliography of significant primary and secondary works by and about Theodore Dreiser published in

---

① Murayama K. "Theodore Dreiser and the Modernists". Studies in American Naturalism, 2016, 11(2): 38-55.

② Mulligan R. "Thomas P. Riggio on Theodore Dreiser Studies". Studies in American Naturalism, 2010, 5(1): 66-78.

③ See M. "'It Was Written That We Meet': The Collaborative Friendship of Theodore Dreiser and George Douglas". Dreiser Studies, 2003, 34(1): 35-57.

④ Dvorak J. "May Calvert: Dreiser's Lifelong Teacher". Dreiser Studies, 2005, 36(2): 3-29.

2004. Works discussed include *Sister Carrie*, *by* Theodore Dreiser; *Americans in Paris: A Literary Anthology*, edited by Adam Gopnik; *American Nautralism*, edited by Harold Bloom; *The Vast and Terrible Drama: American Literary Naturalism in the Late Nineteenth Century*, by Eric Carl Link; and *A Man's Game: Masculinity and the Anti-Aesthetics of American Literary Naturalism*, by John Dudley. [1]

9. Cultural Study

Jude Davies, in "Theodore Dreiser and the Concept of the Social", explores American novelist Theodore Dreiser's interrogation of notions of society and the social as a concept in his literary works. It argues that while Dreiser's novels are often read as cultural histories of American society, it discusses key texts by Dreiser and demonstrates how his writing became a battleground for rival conceptualizations of American society during the 20th century. [2]

Donald Pizer, in "Theodore Dreiser's *An American Tragedy* and 1920s Flapper Culture", presents a literary criticism of the book *An American Tragedy*, by Theodore Dreiser. It highlights how Dreiser used the flapper figure to authenticate American tragedy and the cultural irony during the middle of 1920s. It explores the murder case of Grace Brown-Chester Gillette from 1906 to 1908, and the trial and execution of Grace's lover Chester Gillette. It outlines the characters and their symbolic significance. [3]

---

[1] Smith R W. "A Dreiser Checklist, 2004". Dreiser Studies, 2005, 36(1): 49-54.

[2] Davies J. "Theodore Dreiser and the Concept of the Social". Studies in American Naturalism, 2022, 17(1): 1-25.

[3] Pizer D. "Theodore Dreiser's *An American Tragedy* and 1920s Flapper Culture". Studies in American Naturalism, 2015, 10(2): 123-132.

10. Feminism Study

Jude Davies, in "Women's Agency, Adoption, and Class in Theodore Dreiser's *Delineator* and *Jennie Gerhardt*", focuses on women's agency, adoption, and class in women's magazine *Delineator* and novel *Jennie Gerhardt* by Theodore Dreiser. It mentions that social historians have demonstrated the modernizing influence of Child Rescue and its role in consolidating a racially and economically exclusive middle-class by splitting the category of American motherhood. It also mention Dreiser's editorship in a typical copy of the magazine with the obligatory fashion coverage. ①

Christina van Houten, in "*Jennie Gerhardt*, Domestic Narrative, and Democratic Architecture: Mapping Nineteenth-Century Women's Labor Culture", presents a depiction of labor and capital form the viewpoint of a working girl in the novel *Jennie Gerhardt*, by Theodore Dreiser. Topics discussed include the themes adopted by Dreiser in his fiction; the plot and characters of *Jennie Gerhardt*; and the feminist strand found in Dreiser's works. The influence of democratic ideals, familial structure, socio-economic and political conditions in Columbus, Ohio in Dreiser's works is also discussed. ②

Tracy Lemaster, in "Feminist Thing Theory in *Sister Carrie*", examines feminist thing theory in the novel *Sister Carrie* by Theodore Dreiser. Bill Brown was the creator of thing theory for literary studies. It explores the symbolism of the two prominent objects in the novel, namely, Carrie's rocking chair and Hurstwood's safe. It discusses how Dreiser describes subjectivity in his novel. ③

---

① Davies J. "Women's Agency, Adoption, and Class in Theodore Dreiser's *Delineator* and *Jennie Gerhardt*". Studies in American Naturalism, 2017, 12(2): 141-170.

② Van Houten C. "*Jennie Gerhardt*, Domestic Narrative, and Democratic Architecture: Mapping Nineteenth-Century Women's Labor Culture". Women's Studies, 2015, 44(3): 301-320.

③ Lemaster T. "Feminist Thing Theory in *Sister Carrie*". Studies in American Naturalism, 2009, 4(1): 41-55.

Chapter 10

Jack London

Jack London (1876-1916)

Jack London was a talented writer so caught up in certain myths that they were part of what destroyed him. As the illegitimate son of an impoverished spiritualist, Flora Wellman, London early learned self-reliance. Although he attended high school and, briefly, college, he was largely self-experienced and subsequently wrote about: San Francisco Bay, first as an oyster pirate and then as a member of the State Fish Patrol; the Bering Sea, as an able seaman on a schooner hunting seals; the nation, across which he tramped as a vagabond; Alaska, where he prospected for gold; and California, where eventually he was a wealthy landowner burdened by the problems of maintaining a large ranch. London saw himself as an exemplar for the rage-to-riches story, an Anglo-Saxon superman with superior intelligence and physical press, who took pride in his individualism, yet sympathized with the masses and believed that some form of socialism was the cure for the inequities of capitalism society.

Critical Perspectives

1. Thematic Study

Cara Erdheim Kilgallen, in "Aging Athletes, Broken Bodies, and Disability in Jack London's Prizefighting Prose", focuses on issues regarding aging athletes, broken bodies, and disability in prizefighting prose by Jack London, Klondike stories, nautical adventures, and socialist sentiments. It mentions eugenic sentiments of Anglo-Saxon superiority and socialist concerns for underprivileged people. It also mentions disability studies and naturalist narratives in American sport stories. [1]

2. New-historicism

Clint Pumphrey and Bradford Cole, in "Hurdling the Social Pit: Contextualizing London's *Tramp Diary*", present a literary criticism of the book *The Tramp Diary* by Jack London. Topics discussed include nationwide unemployment demonstrations and self-made businessman; the alleviation of unemployment and the poor treatment of the employed; and the exploration of the historical context. [2]

---

[1] Kilgallen C E. "Aging Athletes, Broken Bodies, and Disability in Jack London's Prizefighting Prose". Studies in American Naturalism, 2017, 12 (2): 200-219.

[2] Pumphrey C, Cole B. "Hurdling the Social Pit: Contextualizing London's *Tramp Diary*". Studies in American Naturalism, 2019, 14(1): 1-18.

3. Psychoanalytical Study

Eric Carl Link, in "The Five Suicides of *Martin Eden*", presents a literary criticism of the book *Martin Eden* by Jack London. It outlines a revealing exchange between two young writers as London confesses to Elwyn Hoffman that his own regrets and anxieties have led him to contemplate suicide on occasion, and he suggests that one way to counter that dark impulse is to get passionate about a topic and give a lecture about it. It also discusses that suicide is one of the central elements or themes driving the plot of the novel *Martin Eden*. [1]

4. Religious Study

Steven Bembridge, in "Jesus as a Cultural Weapon in the Work of Jack London", presents on author Jack London and his integration of Jesus Christ in his work. It provides a brief overview of London's family background, his attitude towards religion, and his conception of Christ over the course of six works, like *The God of His Fathers*, *The People of the Abyss*, and *The Heathen*. It discusses the qualities of Christ that emerge from the changes in American Protestantism during the late 19th and early 20th centuries. [2]

---

[1] Link E C. "The Five Suicides of *Martin Eden*". Studies in American Naturalism, 2018, 13(2): 150-164.

[2] Bembridge S. "Jesus as a Cultural Weapon in the Work of Jack London". Studies in American Naturalism, 2015, 10(1): 22-40.

5. Ecological Study

Aleksandra Hernandez, in "Jack London's Poetic Animality and the Problem of Domestication", argues that Jack London suggests an answer to questions in his imaginative forays into the inner world of dogs. Writing alongside female advocates for the humane treatment of animals, who believed in the reality of animal emotion and reason, London extends the Darwinian tenet that animals differ from humans in degree and not in kind in *Call of the Wild* (1903) and *White Fang* (1906). Attributing cognitive and emotional complexity to animals, he speculates about the impact human domestication practices might have on the quality of their lived experiences. ①

6. Biological Study

Owen Clayton, in "Punks, Prushuns, and Gay-Cats: Vulnerable Youth in the Work of Jack London and A-No. 1", informs about the views of vulnerable youth in the works of Jack London. Topics discussed include several tramp autobiographies; a fictional account of being on the road with London; London's narratives which account specifically the sexual threats faced by transient boys; and male relationships which were often patterned along lines of dominance and submission. ②

---

① Hernandez A. "Jack London's Poetic Animality and the Problem of Domestication". Journal of Modern Literature, 2021, 45(1): 40-55.

② Clayton O. "Punks, Prushuns, and Gay-Cats: Vulnerable Youth in the Work of Jack London and A-No. 1". Studies in American Naturalism, 2019, 14(1): 76-103.

Jay Williams, in "Charmian London's Function in Jack London's Fiction and Nonfiction", talks about literary works by author Jack London whose female characters were at least partly inspired by his wife Charmian Kittredge London. Topics discussed include many of his works talking about the benefits of married life, and his books including *The Valley of the Moon* and *The Little Lady of the Big House*. [1]

Susan Nuernberg and Iris Jamahl Dunkle, in "The Origins of Charmian Kittredge, Jack London's Mate-Woman", discuss the life of Charmian Kittredge before she met and married her husband, author Jack London. Topics discussed include her career as a writer, her early life with parents Dayelle Wiley and Willard Kittredge, and her job as a secretary to Susan Mills, president and business manager of the Mills Seminary and College in Oakland, California. [2]

Iris Jamahl Dunkle, in "Human Document: Charmian London's Role in the Composition of *The Road*", presents a literary criticism of a book *The Road* by Jack London. Topics discussed include London's experiences and development as a writer; his partnership and intellectual collaboration; the tramp as a human character who warranted understanding; and chronological narrative work which focuses on the act of storytelling. [3]

Bruce Watson, in "Jack London Followed His Muse into the Wild", looks at the life of author Jack London, who wrote many well-known books including *The Call of the Wild*. Topics discussed include his childhood; the relationship between

---

[1] Williams J. "Charmian London's Function in Jack London's Fiction and Nonfiction". Women's Studies, 2017, 46(4): 343-361.

[2] Nuernberg S, Dunkle I J. "The Origins of Charmian Kittredge, Jack London's Mate-Woman". Women's Studies, 2017, 46(4): 273-302.

[3] Dunkle I J. "Human Document: Charmian London's Role in the Composition of *The Road*". Studies in American Naturalism, 2019, 14(1): 19-31.

his parents; his days at sea; education; life in Alaska; marriages; his dedication to his writing; physiological effects of all his travels; and his death.①

7. Philosophical Study

Sue Walsh, in "The Child in Wolf's Clothing: The Meanings of the 'Wolf' and Questions of Identity in Jack London's *White Fang*", argues that the criticism of Jack London's work has been dominated by a reliance upon ideas of the "real", the "authentic" and the "archetypal". One of the figures in London's work around which these ideas crystallize is that of the "wolf". This article examines the way the wolf is mobilized both in the criticism of Jack London's work and in an example of the work: the novel *White Fang* (1906). This novel, though it has often been read as clearly delimiting and demarcating the realms of nature and culture, can be read conversely as unpicking the deceptive simplicity of such categories, as troubling essentialist notions of identity (human/animal, male/female, white/Indian) and as engaging with the complexity of the journey in which a "small animal" becomes human-sexual by crossing the infinite divide that separates life from humanity, the biological from the historical.②

8. Ethical Study

Milton Schwebel, in "Jack London: A Case Study of Moral Creativity", seeks to find the roots of London's moral creativity. After identifying the attributes of

---

① Watson B. "Jack London Followed His Muse into the Wild". Smithsonian, 1998, 28(11): 104-113.
② Walsh S. "The Child in Wolf's Clothing: The Meanings of the 'Wolf' and Questions of Identity in Jack London's *White Fang*". European Journal of American Culture, 2013, 32(1): 55-77.

creativity and moral creativity, the article examines the life of London, extracting the features that appear to have made him one of the most prolific and popular American authors and, in particular, committed him to the welfare of the working classes of the world. The article concludes by examining the educational implications of the case study. [1]

9. Cultural Study

Daniel A. Métraux, in "Jack London's Koreans as 'People of the Abyss'", argues that Jack London was America's leading novelist and short story writer at the dawn of the twentieth century. He was also a brilliant essayist, a feature-writing journalist, a crusading socialist, and an impassioned and articulate spokesman for the underclasses. In his essays and in much of his fiction, London was determined to demonstrate the squalid living conditions of the working class. His most poignant work is his 1903 book *The People of the Abyss*, which brilliantly portrays the economic and social misery of the poor living in London's great East End slum. London's thesis is not a condemnation of the wealthy capitalist class per se; instead, he points out the irony that tens of thousands of British subjects were still living and working in conditions of abject degradation in what was supposedly the wealthiest city in the world. London maintained this theme when he traveled to Japan and Korea during the spring of 1904 to report on the Russo-Japanese War for the Hearst newspaper chain. His twenty-two feature articles and accompanying photographs portray the squalor and degradation of the Korean people. As was the

---

[1] Schwebel M. "Jack London: A Case Study of Moral Creativity". Creativity Research Journal, 2009, 21(4): 319-325.

case the previous year in Great Britain, London's goal was not to condemn Korea's ruling class but to showcase the misery of Korea's mammoth lower classes. ①

Daniel A. Métraux, in "Jack London's Influential Role as an Observer of Early Modern Asia", argues that for his novels and short stories, Jack London is regarded as one of America's most popular writers. Less known today is the fact that he was also an astute observer of East Asian politics, societies, and peoples. Working as a journalist for several newspapers and magazines, he filed numerous articles and essays covering the Russo-Japanese War and even foresaw the rise of Japan and China as world powers. This article provides an overview of London's journalistic and literary contributions about Asia, his insights into Asian ethnic and political complexities, and his vision for pan-Asian/American cooperation. ②

10. Feminism Study

Katie O'Donnell Arosteguy, in "'Things Men Must Do': Negotiationg American Masculinity in Jack London's *The Valley of the Moon*", discusses the role of masculinity in Jack London's book *The Valley of the Moon*. The author also examines the argument that London empowered female characters in his works by advocating androgyny and freeing them from sexual attitudes during the time. The article also looks at previous criticism of sexuality in London's work. ③

---

① Métraux D A. "Jack London's Koreans as 'People of the Abyss'". Journal of Global South Studies, 2018, 35(2): 346-358.
② Métraux D A. "Jack London's Influential Role as an Observer of Early Modern Asia". Southeast Review of Asian Studies, 2008(30): 55-66.
③ O'Donnell Arosteguy K. "'Things Men Must Do': Negotiationg American Masculinity in Jack London's *The Valley of the Moon*". Atenea, 2008, 28(1): 37-54.

Chapter 11

Sherwood Anderson

Sherwood Anderson (1876-1941)

In an interview, William Faulkner stated that Sherwood Anderson was "the father of my generation of American writers and the tradition of American writing which our successors will carry on"[①]. Anderson's importance in literary history is accurately summed in Faulkner's statement. Anderson is a seminal figure whose prose style has had a significant impact on the direction of American literature in the 20th century. As a boy from a small town in Ohio, Anderson fell under the spell of Twain's *Huckleberry Finn* with its innocent narrator and non-literary, vernacular style. Later he became fascinated with Gertrude Steins' attempt to use language as a plastic medium, the way an artist uses paints. The influences on Anderson resulted in the development of a simple and concrete style that close to the rhythms of American speech. This style left an indelible imprint on the prose of Hemingway and his followers.

---

① https://paulreuben.website/pal/chap7/anderson.html.

Critical Perspectives

1. Thematic Study

Michael Finnegan, in "*Death in the Woods and Other Stories*: A Closer Look at Sherwood Anderson's Craftsmanship in His Final Book of Tales", focuses on the 1933 short story collection *Death in the Woods and Other Stories*, by American novelist Sherwood Anderson. Topics discussed include the way the personal and professional changes experienced by Anderson which may have influenced the themes of his short stories; the effectiveness of the writing technique of Anderson; and brief details about the plots, characters, and settings of his short stories.[1]

2. New-historicism

Celia Esplugas, in "Sherwood Anderson's *Beyond Desire* and the Industrial South", presents a literary criticism of the novel *Beyond Desire* by U. S. author Sherwood Anderson. The author examines the ways in which Anderson defends Southern U. S. workers' rights and denounces the South's capitalist industrial economic system. The author details the development of Anderson's political activism, emphasizing his belief in communism and involvement in the U. S. labor

---

[1] Finnegan M. "*Death in the Woods and Other Stories*: A Closer Look at Sherwood Anderson's Craftsmanship in His Final Book of Tales". The Midwest Quarterly, 2021, 62(2): 176-188.

movement. The novel's depiction of conflict between the middle-class and mill workers is discussed as well. ①

3. Gender Study

William Holtz, in "Sherwood Anderson and Rose Wilder Lane: Source and Method in *Dark Laughter*", discusses the inspiration and method of portrayal of the Quat'z Arts Ball scene in Sherwood Anderson's *Dark Laughter*. Topics discussed include treatment of the theme of sexual repression in the novel; Freudian insight into the novel; presentation of Anderson's dilemma about life in the novel; and foundation of the character Rose Frank on American journalist Rose Wilder Lane. ②

4. Feminism Study

Celia C. Esplugas, in "María Luisa Bombal and Sherwood Anderson: Early Twentieth-Century Pan-American Feminism(s)", analyzes the feminist perspectives evident in Sherwood Anderson's *Winesburg, Ohio* and María Luisa Bombal's *La última niebla* and *La amortajada*. In their respective cultures, female characters, victimized by fathers and husbands, and constricted by social environments and authoritarian religions, succumb to personal frustration that leads to emotional imbalance and, in some cases, even to the verge of insanity. As scathing critics of their monolithic cultures, both Anderson and Bombal condemn institutional

---

① Esplugas C. "Sherwood Anderson's *Beyond Desire* and the Industrial South". Mississippi Quarterly, 2010, 63(3/4): 655-678.

② Holtz W. "Sherwood Anderson and Rose Wilder Lane: Source and Method in *Dark Laughter*". Journal of Modern Literature, 1985, 12(1): 131-152.

structures that repress women's rights and individual development. As strong advocates of women's full-fledged subjectivity, these authors deconstruct patriarchal cultures and pioneer the advent of women's liberation in their respective societies. The comparative study of these two authors reveals an emergent Pan-American dialectic that continues to demand the deconstruction of patriarchal cultures in today's global societies.[①]

[①] Esplugas C C. "María Luisa Bombal and Sherwood Anderson: Early Twentieth-Century Pan-American Feminism(s)". College Literature, 2013, 40(2): 155-170.

Chapter 12

F. S. Fitzgerald

F. S. Fitzgerald (1896-1940)

Like so many modern American writers, Francis Scott Fitzgerald created a public image of himself as a representative figure of his times, which may have been a part of the promotional campaign to sell his fiction. It worked for a while, with such success that any effort to evoke the Jazz Age or the Roaring Twenties is inevitably accompanied by a reference to or a photograph of Fitzgerald. Public memory is fickle. After he and Zelda had left the big stage and the gossip columnists no longer had their reckless antics to report, people forgot that he was once considered a writer of great promise and talent, and few realized that he had produced a body of work that rings him status as a writer of all times.

Critical Perspectives

1. Thematic Study

Peter L. Hays, in "Oxymoron in *The Great Gatsby*", presents a literary criticism of the book *The Great Gatsby* by F. Scott Fitzgerald. The author discusses oxymoron and paradoxes in the novel such as the doubleness of the character Gatsby's reaction to the character Daisy. The author analyzes other paradoxes in the novel and suggests that Fitzgerald included oxymorons in the novel to reflect contradictions in the national American psyche.[①]

2. New-historicism

Heather L. N. Hess, in "'The Crash!': Writing the Great Depression in F. Scott Fitzgerald's *Babylon Revisited*, *Emotional Bankruptcy*, and *Crazy Sunday*", argues that despite popular critical assumptions that F. Scott Fitzgerald was largely untouched by the stock market crash of 1929, he pays marked attention to it in his ledger, suggesting that he saw the 1929 crash as a landmark not only in America, but in his own life. Furthermore, Fitzgerald's short stories in the early years of the Depression, particularly *Babylon Revisited* (1930), *Emotional Bankruptcy* (1931), and *Crazy Sunday* (1932), reflect the way in which he internalized the trauma of

---

① Hays P L. "Oxymoron in *The Great Gatsby*". Papers on Language and Literature, 2011, 47(3): 318-325.

the Great Depression, reconstituting its economic rhetoric in the description of emotional and psychological phenomena. All three works echo buzzwords like "spend", "pay", "confidence", and "bankruptcy"; employ pivotal moments of crash or collapse; and illustrate the concept of emotional bankruptcy. By analyzing these stories, readers may begin to understand his literary contributions as the writer not only of the American Jazz Age, but of the Great Depression. [1]

Paul Hackman, in "'The Most Important and the Most Difficult Subject for Our Time': Hollywood and *Tender Is the Night*", presents literary criticism of the book *Tender Is the Night* by F. Scott Fitzgerald. It focuses on the relationship between Fitzgerald and the motion picture industry of Hollywood, Los Angeles, California, as manifested in Fitzgerald's literary works as well as biographical accounts including essays and anecdotes. [2]

3. Psychoanalytical Study

Adam Meehan, in "Repetition, Race, and Desire in *The Great Gatsby*", argues that although disagreement persists over exactly what role race plays in *The Great Gatsby*, the issue cannot be ignored, especially in recent critical studies. Yet *Gatsby* reveals an unexplored angle that intersects with psychoanalysis in relation to Lacan's "fundamental fantasy". The protagonist's object of desire, Daisy, is the maternal figure in a (self-)destructive adult repetition of the oedipal drama, complicated by her metaphorical associations with the American landscape and her husband Tom's patriarchal and nativist views. Ultimately, the novel's symbolic

---

[1] Hess H L N. "'The Crash!': Writing the Great Depression in F. Scott Fitzgerald's *Babylon Revisited*, *Emotional Bankruptcy*, and *Crazy Sunday*". Journal of Modern Literature, 2018, 42(1): 77-94.

[2] Hackman P. "'The Most Important and the Most Difficult Subject for Our Time': Hollywood and *Tender Is the Night*". Papers on Language and Literature, 2011, 47(1): 63-87.

structure is haunted by a latent desire to reconstitute Gatsby's ambiguous socially-projected racial makeup as only figuratively white.[1]

4. Gender Study

Alan Bilton, in "Hot Cats and Big Men on Campus: From This Side of Paradise to the Freshman", explores a number of perhaps surprising parallels between Fitzgerald's archetypal campus novel, *This Side of Paradise* (1920), and Harold Lloyd's 1925 parody of the college genre, *The Freshman*. In particular the essay seeks to examine the gendered relationship between the narcissistic self and the crowd, whether in terms of Fitzgerald's view of the positive and negative crowd, or Harold Lloyd's obsession with conformity and belonging. The essay argues that the college genre of the twenties marked a key transition in American culture from older forms of elitism and privilege—identity rooted in aping older modes of distinction and nobility—to new modes of social recognition derived from movies, advertising and consumer goods. It thus explores the "glamour" and hallowed aura attached to college life in the light of American ideas of celebrity and constructed identity, and reads both Fitzgerald's novel and Lloyd's film in terms of a critical engagement with this nascent mode of belonging.[2]

5. Narrative Study

Derek Lee, in "Dark Romantic: F. Scott Fitzgerald and the Specters of Gothic

---

[1] Meehan A. "Repetition, Race, and Desire in *The Great Gatsby*". Journal of Modern Literature, 2014, 37(2): 76-91.

[2] Bilton A. "Hot Cats and Big Men on Campus: From This Side of Paradise to the Freshman". European Journal of American Culture, 2008, 27(2): 93-110.

Modernism", argues that while critics have historically maligned F. Scott Fitzgerald's fantastical writings as side experiments in allegory and nonsense, this unusual set of fictions highlights a previously unrecognized "Gothic mode" that compels us to reinterpret much of his literary corpus. Tracing the archetypal figure of the ghost in *A Short Trip Home*, *The Ice Palace*, *One Trip abroad*, *Thank You for the Light* and *This Side of Paradise* reconfigures our understanding of the unusual presence of supernatural figures in his work, his relationship with Jazz Age social politics, and his engagement with Gothic literary history. Fitzgerald's latent Gothicism not only throws new light on his forgotten short stories and most acclaimed novels, but also positions him as a central figure in the emerging discourse of Gothic modernism. [1]

6. Post-colonial Study

Lorna L. Perez, in "The Impossible Dream: *The Great Gatsby*, *Bodega Dreams* and the Colonial Difference", argues for a reading of Ernesto Quiñonez's novel *Bodega Dreams* as a post-colonial response to F. Scott Fitzgerald's classic Jazz Age novel *The Great Gatsby*. In probing the intertextual connections between the two novels, this paper argues that Quiñonez's engagement with Fitzgerald's text should be read as post-colonial response, as doing so highlights the persistent coloniality that is experienced by Puerto Ricans living in the mainland United States. By reading *Bodega Dreams* within the context of its specific Puerto Rican cultural dynamics, the paper argues that the coloniality of the Puerto Rican diaspora is revealed, and thus amplifies the critique of the American Dream that is initiated in

---

[1] Lee D. "Dark Romantic: F. Scott Fitzgerald and the Specters of Gothic Modernism". Journal of Modern Literature, 2018, 41(4): 125-142.

Fitzgerald's classic.①

Garrett Bridger Gilmore, in "Refracting Blackness: Slavery and Fitzgerald's Historical Consciousness", explores the role of the legacy of slavery in author F. Scott Fitzgerald's sense of American modernity in his mature fiction. Topics discussed include the appearance of slavery in his story *The Diamond as Big as the Ritz* (1922); the whiteness that grounds his historical consciousness; and the racist dynamics exhibited in his novels *The Great Gatsby* and *Tender Is the Night*. Also noted is the mechanism of refraction for expressing historical trauma in social reality.②

7. Biological Study

William J. Quirk, in "Living on $500,000 a Year: What F. Scott Fitzgerald's Tax Returns Reveal about His Life and Times", examines the tax returns of author F. Scott Fitzgerald between 1919 and 1940. Fitzgerald's reputation as a spendthrift is believed to be unjust, as his ledgers have shown him to act under conservative financial principals until his wife Zelda became ill in 1929. The income earned by Fitzgerald through the publication of short stories is compared to his earnings from novels. The author speculates on what Fitzgerald's earnings would be worth in 2009. Fitzgerald's employment as a writer for MGM studios in 1937 and 1938 is discussed.③

---

① Perez L L. "The Impossible Dream: *The Great Gatsby*, *Bodega Dreams* and the Colonial Difference". Centro Journal, 2021, 33(3): 99-127.

② Gilmore G B. "Refracting Blackness: Slavery and Fitzgerald's Historical Consciousness". Mississippi Quarterly, 2017/2018, 70/71(2): 181-203.

③ Quirk W J. "Living on $500,000 a Year: What F. Scott Fitzgerald's Tax Returns Reveal about His Life and Times". The American Scholar, 2009, 78(4): 96-101.

Dorothy Rompalske, in "From Dazzle to Despair: The Short, Brilliant Life of F. Scott Fitzgerald", presents a biography of American writer F. Scott Fitzgerald. Topics discussed include his education experience; his life in the army; his novels and short stories; and his marriage with Zelda Fitzgerald. [1]

Julie M. Irwin, in "F. Scott Fitzgerald's Little Drinking Problem", discusses fiction about alcohol and alcoholism written by F. Scott Fitzgerald. Topics discussed include Fitzgerald's problems with alcoholism; attempts of literature about Fitzgerald to analyze his downfall; and short stories Fitzgerald wrote about drinking which provide the basis for a more intimate understanding of the man and his work. [2]

Joseph Epstein, in "F. Scott Fitzgerald's Third Act", focuses on the novelist F. Scott Fitzgerald and his writings. Topics discussed include his reputation of failure; problem with drunkenness and handling of money; comparison with Ernest Hemingway and William Faulkener; Matthew J. Bruccoli's collection of Fitzgerald's letters; Jeffrey Meyer's biography of Fitzgerald; recognition of his intelligence and imagination; and Fitzgerald's life as a cautionary tale. [3]

Darrel Mansell, in "Self-Disdain in *Tender Is the Night*", delineates the similarities between Richard Diver, the protagonist of *Tender Is the Night*, a novel by F. Scott Fitzgerald, and Fitzgerald himself, his career and view of the world. F. Scott Fitzgerald creates the novel based on an actual person, Gerald Murphy, an acquaintance of Fitzgerald. The novel is about social behavior: the refined, slightly decadent manners of rich American expatriates like the Murphy's good life in Europe between the wars. There is nothing wrong with such a reading; but Dick

---

[1] Rompalske D. "From Dazzle to Despair: The Short, Brilliant Life of F. Scott Fitzgerald". Biography, 1999, 3(3): 102-109.

[2] Irwin J M. "F. Scott Fitzgerald's Little Drinking Problem". The American Scholar, 1987, 56(3): 415-426.

[3] Epstein J. "F. Scott Fitzgerald's Third Act". Commentary, 1994, 98(5): 52-61.

Diver is also very much F. Scott Fitzgerald. There are many similarities between Dick Diver and his author. Reading the novel this way makes it about authorship. Fitzgerald likened his plot to Theodore Dreiser's in *An American Tragedy*. Diver's decline is physical, mental, emotional and spiritual; Fitzgerald even sees in him the decline of the American novel and of American culture. Fitzgerald sees in him also the decline of all these things in himself. Eastward vision for Fitzgerald is the recidivism of culture to its origins in barbarism. Laconic barbarism expresses itself in a new, essentially non-verbal art form, the cinema. The cinema will be the cultural power in the new world—power that once belonged to the world, to Richard Diver and to the novelist F. Scott Fitzgerald.[①]

8. Cultural Study

Sarah Churchwell, in "'$4,000 a Screw': The Prostituted Art of F. Scott Fitzgerald and Ernest Hemingway", argues that F. Scott Fitzgerald and Ernest Hemingway wrote to and about each other from their meeting shortly after the publication of *The Great Gatsby* in 1925, until Hemingway's *A Moveable Feast* was published posthumously in 1964. Their correspondence reveals a consistently deployed sexualized discourse in order to compare anxieties about the relationship of masculinity to commercialism and to art. The code these writers developed enabled them to negotiate shifting power relations as they vied with each other to be the better artist, and the more successful man of business. Trying to reconcile high art with commercialism, they sought to manage conflicting cultural ideologies that declared commerce masculine but vulgar, and art feminine but pure. Mixing the language of the Puritan work ethic with sexual metaphors, they measured their

---

① Mansell D. "Self-Disdain in *Tender Is the Night*". The Midwest Quarterly, 2004, 45(3): 227-239.

success against each other and their culture's shifting definitions of value. The notorious "matter of measurements" episode in *A Moveable Feast* only becomes fully legible when it is read within this history of competitive "measuring". [1]

9. Feminism Study

Leland S. Person Jr., in "Fitzgerald's *O Russet Witch!*: Dangerous Women, Dangerous Art", discusses the short story *O Russet Witch!*, by F. Scott Fitzgerald. It seems to epitomize the female character dualism, while others view it as endemic in American male writing. Topics discussed include polarization of women into goddess and bitch, and the revelation of Fitzgerald's fears about the dangers of male-female relationships and the self-destructive power of his art. [2]

10. Comparative Study

Jessica Martell and Zackary Vernon, in "'Of Great Gabasidy': Joseph Conrad's *Lord Jim* and F. Scott Fitzgerald's *The Great Gatsby*", argue that F. Scott Fitzgerald likely gleaned the title for his magnum opus *The Great Gatsby* from an enigmatic passage in Joseph Conrad's *Lord Jim*, in which the eponymous character is said to be "of great gabasidy"—a polyglot's pronunciation of great capacity. But the parallels between Conrad and Fitzgerald's novels go well beyond the title, most notably in the way that Fitzgerald fashions Gatsby in the image of Jim. Moreover, both Conrad and Fitzgerald meditate on Jim's and Gatsby's

---

[1] Churchwell S. "'$4,000 a Screw': The Prostituted Art of F. Scott Fitzgerald and Ernest Hemingway". European Journal of American Culture, 2005, 24(2): 105-129.

[2] Person L S Jr. "Fitzgerald's *O Russet Witch!*: Dangerous Women, Dangerous Art". Studies in Short Fiction, 1986, 23(4): 443-448.

"capacity", which they imbue with a romantic optimism that forestalls the traumas of the past. Fitzgerald utilizes Conrad and his protagonist as a model for how to place a conventionally romantic character within a text that is otherwise preoccupied with modernist forms and themes.[①]

[①] Martell J, Vernon Z. "'Of Great Gabasidy': Joseph Conrad's *Lord Jim* and F. Scott Fitzgerald's *The Great Gatsby*". Journal of Modern Literature, 2015, 38(3): 56-70.

Chapter 13

Ernest Hemingway

Ernest Hemingway (1899-1961)

When Ernest Hemingway was awarded the Nobel Prize for Literature, the Swedish Academy commented on the central themes of his work. Courage and compassion in a world of violence and death were seen as the distinguishing marks of "one of the great writers of our time—who, honestly and undauntedly, reproduces the genuine features of the hard utterance of the age". These comments sum up perceptively the characteristic preoccupation of Hemingway's fiction and of the heroic code of behavior which it explores. Hemingway was also a careful artist, for whom every book was, in his own words, "a new beginning", in which the writer "should always try for something that has never been done". [1]

---

[1] https://www.brainyquote.com/quotes/ernest_hemingway_714949.

Critical Perspectives

1. New-historicism

Jeff Morgan, in "Hemingway and the Cuban Revolution: *For Whom the Bell Tolls* in the Sierra Maestra", explores the Cuban Revolution in Ernest Hemingway's 1940 novel *For Whom the Bell Tolls*. Topics discussed include the connection between Cuban leader Fidel Castro and Hemingway; the difficulty of correlating the guerilla action during the Cuban Revolution with the action depicted by Hemingway in the novel; and the existential work ethic evident in the book.[①]

Danell Ragsdell-Hetrick, in "Catherine, the Baby and the Gas: The Fatal Effects of Twilight Sleep in *A Farewell to Arms*", explores the death of an infant and mother during childbirth in the book *A Farewell to Arms*, by author Ernest Hemingway. It is suggested that they were victims of the anesthetic medical practice of scopolamine-morphine narcosis (Twilight Sleep). Other topics include pain control during labor; the dangers of modern medicine; and administration of anesthetics.[②]

Alex A. Cardoni, in "Medicine and Medicines in Hemingway's Arkansas", explores the role of illness, medicinal drugs, and home remedies in the writing of U.S. author Ernest Hemingway. The author reflects on his marriage to wife Pauline

---

① Morgan J. "Hemingway and the Cuban Revolution: *For Whom the Bell Tolls* in the Sierra Maestra". War, Literature and the Arts: An International Journal of the Humanities, 2016(28): 1-12.

② Ragsdell-Hetrick D. "Catherine, the Baby and the Gas: The Fatal Effects of Twilight Sleep in *A Farewell to Arms*". Arkansas Review: A Journal of Delta Studies, 2014, 45(2): 115-119.

Pfeiffer and her family's ownership of Pfeiffer Chemical Company (Pfeiffer Pharmaceuticals). Stories noted include *A Simple Enquiry*, *A Natural History of the Dead*, and *The Snows of Kilimanjaro*.①

2. Psychoanalytical Study

Zennure Köseman, in "James Joyce's Manifestation of Epiphany in Ernest Hemingway's *Big Two-Hearted River*", highlights that Ernest Hemingway's main character, Nick Adams, acquires an epiphany of natural healing by returning to his childhood fishing terrains. Hemingway specifies the terrifying reality of World War I through Nick Adams' having a psychological disturbance from the war by reflecting nature's profound healing source in *Big Two-Hearted River*. Following his return, Nick Adams overcomes the battle disturbances psychologically by diving into the natural fishing area. When he visits his previous fishing environment, he revives himself from terrible war memories. His escape into nature implies that he, thereby, is the lover of nature. Through the acquisition of natural healing in his childhood fishing areas, Hemingway, concurrently, manifests James Joyce's epiphany in his target short story. Nick Adams becomes relaxed while possessing a peaceful mind in natural living. Therefore, this article, being interested in Nick Adams' thinking and diving into his previous living areas, focuses on how he has a maturity within himself in nature.②

Christopher D. Martin, in "Ernest Hemingway: A Psychological Autopsy of a Suicide", argues that much has been written about Ernest Hemingway, including

---

① Cardoni A A. "Medicine and Medicines in Hemingway's Arkansas". Arkansas Review: A Journal of Delta Studies, 2014, 45(2): 104-112.

② Köseman Z. "James Joyce's Manifestation of Epiphany in Ernest Hemingway's *Big Two-Hearted River*". Gaziantep University Journal of Social Sciences, 2021, 20 (4): 1795-1804.

discussion of his well-documented mood disorder, alcoholism, and suicide. However, a thorough biopsychosocial approach capable of integrating the various threads of the author's complex psychiatric picture has yet to be applied. Application of such a psychiatric view to the case of Ernest Hemingway in an effort toward better understanding of the author's experience with illness and the tragic outcome is the aim of this investigation. Thus, Hemingway's life is examined through a review and discussion of biographies, psychiatric literature, personal correspondence, photography, and medical records. Significant evidence exists to support the diagnoses of bipolar disorder, alcohol dependence, traumatic brain injury, and probable borderline and narcissistic personality traits. Late in life, Hemingway also developed symptoms of psychosis likely related to his underlying affective illness, superimposed alcoholism and traumatic brain injury. Hemingway utilized a variety of defense mechanisms, including self-medication with alcohol, a lifestyle of aggressive, risk-taking sportsmanship, and writing, in order to cope with the suffering caused by the complex comorbidity of his interrelated psychiatric disorders. Ultimately, Hemingway's defense mechanisms failed, overwhelmed by the burden of his complex comorbid illness, resulting in his suicide. However, despite suffering from multiple psychiatric disorders, Hemingway was able to live a vibrant life until the age of 61 and within that time contributed immortal works of fiction to the literary canon.[①]

3. Gender Study

Larry Grimes, in "Echoes and Influences: A Comparative Study of Short Fiction by Ernest Hemingway and Robert Morgan", presents literary criticism on the

---

[①] Martin C D. "Ernest Hemingway: A Psychological Autopsy of a Suicide". Psychiatry: Interpersonal and Biological Processes, 2006, 69(4): 351-361.

short fiction of American authors Ernest Hemingway and Robert Morgan. The author analyzes Hemingway's influence in five stories from Morgan's 1999 collection *The Balm of Gilead Tree*. The depictions of Native Americans and gender roles in both authors' work are examined. The article also provides a critical interpretation of Morgan's depiction of the U. S. Civil War. [1]

4. Narrative Study

William Cain, in "Sentencing: Hemingway's Aesthetic", argues that Ernest Hemingway's aesthetic—a better term than style—is based on constant acts of choice and decisions that he makes as a writer at every moment about which word and phrase to set down on the page. All writers must make choices—what to include, what to exclude. Hemingway is special because his work as a writer foregrounds this fact. The structure of Hemingway's sentences makes the reader keenly aware of the words that he has selected and, just as much or more, the countless other possibilities that he has not selected. Hemingway first presented and developed his aesthetic in his major novels and short stories of the 1920s. But this high level of achievement proved very difficult for Hemingway to sustain in the decades that followed. The story of his aesthetic and the shape of his literary career are triumphant and tragic. [2]

5. Religious Study

George Monteiro, in "Ernest Hemingway, Psalmist", explores author Ernest

---

[1] Grimes L. "Echoes and Influences: A Comparative Study of Short Fiction by Ernest Hemingway and Robert Morgan". The Southern Quarterly, 2010, 47(3): 98-116.

[2] Cain W. "Sentencing: Hemingway's Aesthetic". Society, 2015, 52(1): 80-85.

Hemingway's reading of Biblical text, King David's *Twenty-Third Psalm*, and its effect on his writings in the late 1920s and early 1930s. Topics discussed include background on the subject of Ernest Hemingway and the Bible; details of an examination of Hemingway manuscript and typescript at the John F. Kennedy Library; and famous Bible-inspired books of Hemingway. ①

6. Canonization Study

Mel Kenne, in "Dirty, White Candles: Ernest Hemingway's Encounter with the East", considers the ways in which the experience of Turkey has shaped the imaginations of American writer Ernest Hemingway. In the fall of 1922, Hemingway visited Istanbul to cover the end of the Greco-Turkish War and its aftermath. Hemingway noted in his October 18, 1922 dispatch about the dirtiness of the city, comparing the minarets to dirty, white candles. Hemingway's past and present political conflicts involving Turkey and Greece are explored. ②

7. Biological Study

Eric M. Poeschla, in "Hemingway's Last Letter", presents a letter written by author Ernest Hemingway before his death about surroundings of Rochester, Minnesota and his last days. It discusses surroundings of Rochester including skull sculptures of animals, games outside shops and river valleys. Other topics discussed include Hemingway's depression of not writing, the author's suicide by shotgun

---

① Monteiro G. "Ernest Hemingway, Psalmist". Journal of Modern Literature, 1987, 14(1): 83-95.

② Kenne M. "Dirty, White Candles: Ernest Hemingway's Encounter with the East". Texas Studies in Literature and Language, 2012, 54(4): 494-504.

and the Dakota War in 1862. [1]

Jeffrey Meyers, in "Hemingway & Malraux: The Struggle", reflects upon the writers Ernest Hemingway and André Malraux. Particular focus is given to how the authors had hostile and combative relations. Various similarities between the authors are also discussed, including their affinity for cats, their struggles with mental health, their writing practices and their romantic lives. [2]

Jason Holt, in "Hemingway's Death in *The Sun Also Rises*", regards the death of author Ernest Hemingway in the U.S. It outlines the author's investigation on Hemingway's intention of committing suicide and the significance of his novels. The author also describes Hemingway's character as a person and novelist, and how he died from literary determination. [3]

8. Philosophical Study

Zennure Köseman, in "Various Meaningfulness in Ernest Hemingway's Short-Short Story *For Sale: Baby Shoes, Never Worn*", aims to study the contemporary literary genre, short short story, also known as micro fiction or flash fiction. It draws people's attention to what is hidden rather than what is visible. This literary analysis highlights that various meaningfulness is acquired when short short stories are handled in respect to readers' different critical evaluations. As short short stories attain new meanings in different interpretations because of having implicit and open-ended structures, they should be considered in terms of deconstructive analysis and the perceptional aesthetics reflecting reading public's mood towards the text.

---

[1] Poeschla E M. "Hemingway's Last Letter". Southwest Review, 2015, 100(1): 100-112.
[2] Meyers J. "Hemingway & Malraux: The Struggle". The New Criterion, 2015, 34(3): 75-80.
[3] Holt J. "Hemingway's Death in *The Sun Also Rises*". Pennsylvania Literary Journal, 2013, 5(2): 37-40.

This article focuses on Ernest Hemingway's short short story, *For Sale: Baby Shoes, Never Worn*, in terms of various meaningfulness that implies what is hidden rather than what is seen. [1]

David Sears, in "The Fighter and the Writer", shares the story of the comradeship of U. S. Colonel Charles T. Lanham of the 22nd Infantry Regiment and then war correspondent Ernest Hemingway in 1944 on Europe's battlefields. Historical information is provided about the job of Hemingway. [2]

Timo Müller, in "The Uses of Authenticity: Hemingway and the Literary Field, 1926-1936", argues that authenticity is a widespread but ambiguous notion in our collective imagination. Cut off from its essentialist roots by various schools of twentieth-century philosophy, it has come to be shaped, as a discursive construct, by popular culture rather than scholarly thought. This article examines selected works of Ernest Hemingway, who became one of the most influential creators and arbiters of authenticity in modern (popular) literature but who constantly subjected the concept to critical scrutiny in his fiction. This ambivalent attitude grew out of Hemingway's interaction with the modernist literary field. Initially, posturing as an authentic writer served to distinguish him from the urban bohème. Later, as the posture became fashionable and threatened to lose its distinctive function, he questioned and refined it on a regular basis in his works, which thus allows us a glimpse at the collective imagination of authenticity in the making. [3]

Ron McFarland, in "The World's Most Interesting Man", focuses on the author Ernest Hemingway, including the novel *Hemingsteen* by Michael Murphy, *Rhino Ritz: An American Mystery with Ernest Hemingway, Gertrude Stein, & Friends*

---

[1] Köseman Z. "Various Meaningfulness in Ernest Hemingway's Short-Short Story *For Sale: Baby Shoes, Never Worn*". Journal of Graduate School of Social Sciences, 2013, 17(3): 105-116.

[2] Sears D. "The Fighter and the Writer". World War II, 2020, 35(1): 34-41.

[3] Müller T. "The Uses of Authenticity: Hemingway and the Literary Field, 1926-1936". Journal of Modern Literature, 2009, 33(1): 28-42.

by Keith Abbott, and the biography *Hemingway* by Kenneth S. Lynn. An overview of the aforementioned literature's incorporation of fiction into the portraying Hemingway's life is provided. ①

9. Ethical Study

Anita Duneer, in "Last Stands and Frontier Justice", presents a literary criticism of works *The Sea-Wolf* and *A Son of the Sun* by Jack London and works by Ernest Hemingway, *To Have and Have Not*, *The Old Man and the Sea*, and *Islands in the Stream*, which explores the attributes of individualism, self-reliance and physical prowess. Topics discussed include works of the authors on violence and vigilantism which tests the codes of ethics and creates conflicts between natural and civil laws; lack of similarities between the novels of the authors on sea; and efforts of the authors to dramatize the threat of civilization of sea and islands. ②

10. Cultural Study

Eric Gary Anderson and Melanie Benson Taylor, in "The Landscape of Disaster: Hemingway, Porter, and the Soundings of Indigenous Silence", trace the largely unmapped spaces between Ernest Hemingway and Katherine Anne Porter, and make visible the similarly underinvestigated spaces between modernism, Native America, and the circum-Caribbean South. In placing these two important writers in

---

① McFarland R. "The World's Most Interesting Man". The Midwest Quarterly, 2013, 54(4): 414-430.

② Duneer A. "Last Stands and Frontier Justice". Studies in American Naturalism, 2016, 11(1): 23-42.

conversation, this essay demonstrates that the synergy between them expands and complicates a southern studies that has paid them either too little or too much attention, and gives readers fresh ways of thinking about modernism's uneven and often unreflective relationship with Native America.[①]

[①] Anderson E G, Taylor M B. "The Landscape of Disaster: Hemingway, Porter, and the Soundings of Indigenous Silence". Texas Studies in Literature and Language, 2017, 59(3): 319-352.

Chapter 14

William Faulkner

William Faulkner(1897-1962)

William Faulkner often said the regarded poetry as the most difficult genre and himself as a failed pet. Although he wrote prose at early age, he devoted most of his energy as a beginning writer to verse, imitating Husman and Swinburne, translating French Symbolist poets, and coming under the spell of Pound and Eliot. *The Marble Faun*, however, was a cycle of pastoral poems, and one of the keys to both the complexity and power of his mature rose is the carryover of poetic techniques and pastoral imagery in his realistic fiction. In his wasteland novel, *Soldiers' Pay*, he struck the contemporary note of postwar disillusionment. Then he set his scene in Mississippi and began to mine the resources of his native region.

Critical Perspectives

1. Thematic Study

Barbara Ladd, in "Salomé in the Jazz Age: Faulkner, *The Marionettes*, and *Sanctuary*", explores the fascination of authors, particularly William Faulkner, in the depiction of biblical character Salomé in the American Jazz Age. Topics discussed include the enthusiasm demonstrated by Faulkner for fin-de-siècle and literary modernism; the dream sequence presented by Faulkner in his 1920 play *The Marionettes*; and the observations on the themes and characters of his novels, *Sanctuary*, *The Sound and the Fury*, and *As I Lay Dying*.[①]

Philip Sayers, in "'Just One Thing More': *Absalom, Absalom!* and the Creditor-Debtor Relationship", argues that to some extent, art can provide people with a way of thinking outside of the creditor-debtor relationship. This article looks to William Faulkner's *Absalom, Absalom!* (1936) for an answer. It demonstrates, through a reading of the novel's anonymous lawyer, the extent to which the economic logic of the ledger (as a figure for the creditor-debtor relationship) penetrates the novel and its logic of storytelling. The article then goes on to examine, via an analysis of the novel's ending, two "remainders"—two elements that cannot be integrated into this economic logic. Finally, the author of this article draws on Judith Butler's work to suggest that *Absalom, Absalom!* does gesture toward a form of relationality outside of the economic terms of debit and credit, seen

---

[①] Ladd B. "Salomé in the Jazz Age: Faulkner, *The Marionettes*, and *Sanctuary*". Mississippi Quarterly, 2019, 72(1): 25-48.

in Miss Coldfield's initial framing of her tale and in Butler's idea of "dependency". ①

2. New-historicism

Jay Watson, in "So Easy Even a Child Can Do It: William Faulkner's Southern Gothicizers", explores the contribution of American author William Faulkner to the conceptualization of the Southern Gothic genre in the American South literature. Topics discussed include the way novelist Ellen Glasgow acknowledged the Southern Gothic literary works of Faulkner in her 1935 essay *Heroes and Monsters*, and the depiction of cruelty in Faulkner's 1931 novel *Sanctuary*, and 1936 novel *Absalom, Absalom!*, which featured American South families. ②

Wanda Raiford, in "Fantasy and Haiti's Erasure in William Faulkner's *Absalom, Absalom!*", critiques the 1936 novel *Absalom, Absalom!* by William Faulkner, focusing on how the author incorporates the Haitian revolutionary war of independence into the story. It discusses the criticisms against Faulkner for allegedly erasing the significant part of Haitian history from his narrative and speculates on whether the omission was intentional. It also deals with the ways in which the fantasy genre is used by some authors to modify the representation of slavery in literature. ③

---

① Sayers P. "'Just One Thing More': *Absalom, Absalom!* and the Creditor-Debtor Relationship". Canadian Review of American Studies, 2017, 47(2): 219-238.
② Watson J. "So Easy Even a Child Can Do It: William Faulkner's Southern Gothicizers". Mississippi Quarterly, 2019, 72(1): 1-23.
③ Raiford W. "Fantasy and Haiti's Erasure in William Faulkner's *Absalom, Absalom!*". South: A Scholarly Journal, 2016, 49(1): 101-121.

Lisa Klarr, in "Decaying Spaces: Faulkner's Gothic and the Construction of the National Real", discusses the decaying spaces in the U. S. South in the novels of author William Faulkner. Also cited are the ruins of large plantation houses in the 1929 novel *Sartoris* (*Flags in the Dust*), how the ruined barns reflected the shift to industrialized farming in the novel, and some other Faulkner works like *Absalom Absalom!*, *Light in August*, and *The Unvanquished*. [1]

3. Psychoanalytical Study

Phillip Gordon, in "Faulkner in a Time of Pandemic: Tracing the Influence of the 1918 Influenza in His Works", discusses the influence of the 1918 influenza pandemic in the works of author William Faulkner. Also cited are the claim by author Alfred Crosby that the pandemic was never tackled by Faulkner in his writings, the death of Victoria Oldham, a sister of Faulkner's wife Estelle, due to the pandemic, and the impacts of the pandemic to Faulkner's family and home territory in Mississippi. [2]

Michael Swacha, in "Fragmentation, Relationality, and the Possibility of Form: Reconsidering Darl in Faulkner's *As I Lay Dying*", focuses on the pervasive fragmentation in the novel *As I Lay Dying* by William Faulkner and proposes that the fragmentation is not just a reflection of the mental state of the characters but also speaks to the structures of interconnection that pervade our experiences of being. Topics include the concept of relationality; the exploration of relationality as

---

[1] Klarr L. "Decaying Spaces: Faulkner's Gothic and the Construction of the National Real". Mississippi Quarterly, 2019, 72(3): 407-425.

[2] Gordon P. "Faulkner in a Time of Pandemic: Tracing the Influence of the 1918 Influenza in His Works". Mississippi Quarterly, 2019, 72(4): 467-483.

fundamental to our experience of being; and the troubling component of illegibility as a site of utopian imaginings. ①

4. Gender Study

Thea J. Autry, in "'As out of a Seer's Crystal Ball': The Racialized Gaze in William Faulkner's *Intruder in the Dust*", presents a literary criticism of the book *Intruder in the Dust* by William Faulkner. It outlines the characters and explores their symbolic significance which is presented as a figure of masculinity. It examines story of the book as a detective fiction and discusses its racial bildungsroman, transcendence and myths. An overview of the story is also given. ②

5. Marxism Study

Kevin G. Wilson, in "Crisis, Mimetic Desire, and Communal Violence in William Faulkner's *Sanctuary*", presents a literary criticism of the novel *Sanctuary*, by American writer William Faulkner. It outlines the characters and explores the concept of social class, the rape and abduction on college girls in Mississippi, and patriarchy. Information regarding the lack of Christian mercy, and communal violence, is also mentioned. ③

---

① Swacha M. "Fragmentation, Relationality, and the Possibility of Form: Reconsidering Darl in Faulkner's *As I Lay Dying*". The Faulkner Journal, 2019, 33(1): 39-64.
② Autry T J. "'As out of a Seer's Crystal Ball': The Racialized Gaze in William Faulkner's *Intruder in the Dust*". The Faulkner Journal, 2016, 30(2): 19-39.
③ Wilson K G. "Crisis, Mimetic Desire, and Communal Violence in William Faulkner's *Sanctuary*". The Faulkner Journal, 2015, 29(1): 49-69.

6. Narrative Study

Aliz Farkas, in "The Critical Reception of William Faulkner's *The Sound and the Fury* across Time", explores the changes that occurred in the critical reception of Faulkner's *The Sound and the Fury*, which, after a long period of neglect, by now has become his most widely discussed work among literary critics. The author of this essay focuses on three historically and geographically distinct moments in the critical history of the novel: its reception at the time of its first publication in 1929 by the American reading public; American literary criticism written in the 1950's, when more extensive discussions of the work started to appear; and the reception of the novel by the Romanian reading public after 1971, when the Romanian translation was published. Drawing on Hans Robert Jauss's aesthetic of reception, this article seeks to answer two questions with regard to the critical reception of the novel. First, It would like to see whether the literary career of *The Sound and the Fury* follows the trajectory from initial rejection to wide acceptance with increasing aesthetic value, as predicted by Jauss's theory. Second, the author of this article is interested in finding out whether those features of the novel that were initially perceived as unfamiliar and incomprehensible were indeed incorporated into the later readers' horizon of expectations, so that they no longer posed problems for later readers.①

Sarah E. Stunden, in "'Room to Breathe': Narrative Anacrhony and Suffocation in William Faulkner's *Pantaloon in Black*", presents a literary criticism of the book *Go Down, Moses* by American writer William Faulkner. It

---

① Farkas A. "The Critical Reception of William Faulkner's *The Sound and the Fury* across Time". Bulletin of the Transilvania University of Brasov, Series IV: Philology & Cultural Studies, 2017 (2): 53-66.

outlines the characters and explores their symbolic significance. Special focus is given to the short story *Pantaloon in Black*. ①

Astrid Maes, in "No 'Great Truths of the Heart': The Postmodern Hopelessness of *Sanctuary*", discusses William Faulkner's relationship to postmodernism and focuses on his novel *Sanctuary*. The article argues that *Sanctuary* may be seen as a postmodern work due to its sensationalist content, and suggests that Faulkner's modernist practices fail in the face of the commercial logic that pervades *Sanctuary*, making it a novel of silence, doubt, and indeterminacy of language. ②

7. Post-colonial Study

Chiaki Kayaba, in "Inadequate Compensation: Economic Agency against the Plantation System in Faulkner's *Go down, Moses*", argues that the idea of cash payments to African Americans has been seriously discussed as a feasible way to make reparations for slavery. However, *Go down, Moses* (1942) suggests the inadequacy of monetary reparations by depicting the troubled relationship between former slave owners and their unacknowledged black relatives in the Southern plantation. Reading the economic exchanges between the two races in the novel reveals not only an institutional violence that still manipulates blacks' (physical) properties in the postbellum era, but also the agency of black characters who struggle in the white-centered plantation system. This interpretation sheds light on multiple black perspectives that discussions of monetary reparations often ignore. Ultimately, Faulkner's *Go down, Moses* critiques the one-sidedness of modern

---

① Stunden S E. "'Room to Breathe': Narrative Anacrhony and Suffocation in William Faulkner's *Pantaloon in Black*". The Faulkner Journal, 2015, 29(2): 49-69.

② Maes A. "No 'Great Truths of the Heart': The Postmodern Hopelessness of *Sanctuary*". The Faulkner Journal, 2019, 33(1): 93-110.

attempts at racial reconciliation by describing an ethics that originated in blacks' politically complicated interests. ①

Ellen Bonds, in "An 'Other' Look at William Faulkner's *That Evening Sun*", explains the creation of the other, or the process of marginalizing African Americans, in the short story *That Evening Sun*, by William Faulkner. It examines the effect of racist ideology on the mind, imagination and behavior of slaves and masters as depicted in the story. It considers various points of view offered by the story to understand it as an illustration of how children learn racism, racial division or racial discrimination. ②

Sara Gerend, in "'My Son, My Son!': Paternalism, Haiti, and Early Twentieth-Century American Imperialism in William Faulkner's *Absalom, Absalom!*", discusses Maritza Stanchich's and Barbara Ladd's examinations on early twentieth-century U.S. imperialist representations of Haiti in *Absalom, Absalom!*. It notes that William Faulkner's novel foregrounds the design of early 20th-century American empire toward Haiti through paternalism. It emphasizes that the widespread representation of American culture has provided part of the literature empire that help U.S. citizens to learn about the country's conduct in Caribbean affairs. ③

8. Ethical Study

Marco Motta, in "What Can We Learn from Children?: A Reading of *The*

---

① Kayaba C. "Inadequate Compensation: Economic Agency against the Plantation System in Faulkner's *Go down, Moses*". Journal of Modern Literature, 2021, 44(4): 57-72.

② Bonds E. "An 'Other' Look at William Faulkner's *That Evening Sun*". Studies in Short Fiction, 2012, 37(1): 59-68.

③ Gerend S. "'My Son, My Son!': Paternalism, Haiti, and Early Twentieth-Century American Imperialism in William Faulkner's *Absalom, Absalom!*". The Southern Literary Journal, 2009, 42(1): 17-31.

Sound and the Fury", discusses how a novel can make us see children as active and direct witnesses of their time. Through a close reading of *The Sound and the Fury*, the author of this essay asks what adults and scholars can learn from children. By closely looking at the picture of the ordinary through the lens of Faulkner's children recounting household events, the author shows that they can inspire us to look differently at the world and teach us something about human attention and responsiveness to the life of others.①

Thomas Claviez, in "The Southern Demiurge at Work: Modernism, Literary Theory and William Faulkner's *Dry September*", argues that "In light of the increasing politicization that can be observed within the discipline of American Studies in the U.S.—with its focus on race, class and gender—and the neglect of matters aesthetic that more often than not accompanies this phenomenon, canonized modernist texts have been cast under something close to a general suspicion". This development, however, has to be seen in the larger context of academic politics, which is provided in François Cusset's book *French Theory: How Foucault, Derrida, Deleuze, & Co. Transformed the Intellectual Life in the United States* (2008). In it, he diagnoses a split of French post-structuralism into two camps: a school of apolitical textual deconstruction and one of re-politicization based upon identity politics. With the help of a new reading of William Faulkner's short story *Dry September*, the author of this essay argues that this split is both artificial and questionable. The author of this essay also shows that, far from being historically irrelevant or purely mandarin, the aesthetic complexity of modernist texts does not forego but actively addresses the dangers involved in readings motivated by political agendas such as race and gender.②

---

① Motta M. "What Can We Learn from Children?: A Reading of *The Sound and the Fury*". Critical Horizons, 2023, 24(1): 60-75.

② Claviez T. "The Southern Demiurge at Work: Modernism, Literary Theory and William Faulkner's *Dry September*". Journal of Modern Literature, 2009, 32(4): 22-33.

9. Cultural Study

Susan V. Donaldson, in "Flipping the Script: Thadious Davis's Reconstruction of William Faulkner and the South", discusses the impact of author Thadious Davis on the revision, expansion, and reconstruction of the scholarship of author William Faulkner and U.S. Southern cultural studies. Topics discussed include information on Davis's first book *Faulkner's Negro: Art and the Southern Context* (*Southern Literary Studies*) and an overview of Davis's second book *Games of Property: Law, Race, Gender, and Faulkner's "Go down, Moses"*.①

Juliane Schallau, in "Texts of the Sons: William Faulkner, Günter Grass, and the Narration of Guilt", provides an overview of author William Faulkner's works on post-war Germany's violent and guilt-ridden past. It mentions that Faulkner prompted a generation of sons whose texts contributed greatly to the formation of German commemorative culture and to the sons who admitted the collective guilt of the fathers in German post-war society. It also offers comparison of Faulkner's Quentin Compson with Grass's Oskar Mazerath in *The Tin Drum*.②

Richard C. Moreland, in "Forward Movement: William Faulkner's *Letter to the North*, W. E. B. Du Bois's Challenge, and *The Reivers*", focuses on a letter written by U.S. writer William Faulkner to U.S. historian W. E. B. Du Bois. It mentions that challenges by Du Bois seem to have contributed to significant changes in how Faulkner was coming to terms with the Civil Rights Movement and possibilities of social change, including changes in what Jean-Paul Sartre had described in 1939 as

---

① Donaldson S V. "Flipping the Script: Thadious Davis's Reconstruction of William Faulkner and the South". Women's Studies, 2019, 48(6): 587-592.

② Schallau J. "Texts of the Sons: William Faulkner, Günter Grass, and the Narration of Guilt". The Faulkner Journal, 2018, 32(1): 67-87.

Faulkner's metaphysic of time.①

Erin Penner, in "Modernist Moonlight: Illuminating the Postwar Dread of *Flags in the Dust*", discusses how author William Faulkner used the moonlight to symbolize modern warfare like nighttime air raids in his novel *Flags in the Dust*. Also cited are how moonlit air raids became fixtures of modern warfare, his experience with the lost cause narrative, and how Paul K. Saint-Amour explained the devastation of modern warfare that could result in greater civilian deaths.②

10. Feminism Study

Ahmed Honeini, in "'My Poor Little Girl': *Lolita* and Nabokov's Faulkner", focuses on the literary tastes of Vladimir Nabokov and his disdain for William Faulkner. The article argues that key aspects of the main character's personality and actions in *Lolita* are comparable to and a distillation of the characters in Faulkner's novels while also highlighting the similarities in Nabokov and Faulkner's concerns with the abuse and subjugation of women.③

11. Spatial Study

Anne Hirsch Moffitt, in "The City Specter: William Faulkner and the Threat of Urban Encroachment", talks about novels of William Faulkner. The author examines Faulkner's dialogic representation of urbanism and regionalism as a struggle that

---

① Moreland R C. "Forward Movement: William Faulkner's *Letter to the North*, W. E. B. Du Bois's Challenge, and *The Reivers*". The Faulkner Journal, 2016, 30(1): 79-104.
② Penner E. "Modernist Moonlight: Illuminating the Postwar Dread of *Flags in the Dust*". Mississippi Quarterly, 2019, 72(4): 503-520.
③ Honeini A. "'My Poor Little Girl': *Lolita* and Nabokov's Faulkner". The Faulkner Journal, 2019, 33(1): 65-91.

evokes aspects of urban growth. Works examined include the novels *Go down*, *Moses*, *The Sound and the Fury*, and *As I Lay Dying*. Topics include the settings of Northern and Southern U. S. cities in Faulkner's work; the imaginary Yoknapatawpha County; and rural isolation in the short story *Delta Autumn*.[①]

---

① Moffitt A H. "The City Specter: William Faulkner and the Threat of Urban Encroachment". The Faulkner Journal, 2012, 26(1): 17-36.

Chapter 15

Katherine Anne Porter

Katherine Anne Porter (1890-1980)

Katherine Anne Porter was probably the finest writer of short stories and novellas of her time in the United States. Her last work of fiction, *Ship of Fools*, suggests either that the novel as such was not her form, or that the hatred and contempt around in her, by which the German behavior under the Nazis had robbed her both of her usual skill and of her usual sense that life, in all its sadness and frustrations, is incurably poetic. Her collections of essays, *The Days Before*, however, is fascinating both in the excellence of its criticism and in the light it throws on her own: "I am passionately involved with those individuals who populate all these enormous migrations, calamities, who fight wars and furnish life for the future."[①] We see such an individual in Porter's own stories as a quiet, imaginative, sad girl of old southern family, aware of the past because of her grandmother and her old black servant, aware of the grotesque because of a visit to a circus wise clowns frighten her,

---

① https://www.jstor.org/stable/812773.

and aware of death and horror because of a brother who kills a pregnant rabbit and shows her the baby rabbits, who will now never be born in its womb. Porter's great gift as a storyteller is to take material, particularly a wistfulness for the past, a sense of the strangeness, loneliness, cruelty, and treachery of life, the decay of love, or the failure to be able to love, and to avoid the twin temptations of treating this material with other sentimentality or a cheap cynicism.

Critical Perspectives

1. Thematic Study

Sari Edelstein, in "'Pretty as Pictures': Family Photography and Southern Postmemory in Porter's *Old Mortality*", discusses the book *Old Mortality* by Katherine Anne Porter. *Old Mortality* narrates the coming of age of Miranda Grey and reoccurring character in Porter's work. Through Miranda, Porter exemplifies the problems southerners still have struggling with forgetting slavery, the civil war, and most of all, the loss of culture. Porter's story illustrates the post memorable condition of modern southern life. [①]

2. New-historicism

Kodai Iuchi, in "Katherine Anne Porter's Faithful and Relentless Vision of Death in *Pale Horse, Pale Rider*", presents a literary criticism of the novel *Pale Horse, Pale Rider* by Katherine Anne Porter. It explores the interconnected stories that are permeated with a romanticized glorification of death. It shows Southern culture emerging from the Civil War. It discusses the importance of the "storytelling of death" and "discourse of death" as demonstrated by the obsession of Southern

---

① Edelstein S. "'Pretty as Pictures': Family Photography and Southern Postmemory in Porter's *Old Mortality*". The Southern Literary Journal, 2008, 40(2): 151-165.

families with the superiority of the dead ones and the region's past history. ①

David A. Davis, in "The Forgotten Apocalypse: Katherine Anne Porter's *Pale Horse, Pale Rider*, Traumatic Memory, and the Influenza Pandemic of 1918", presents a literary criticism of the book *Pale Horse, Pale Rider* by Katherine Anne Porter. It discusses the interplay between death and memory in the novel. It states that Porter's allusion to the apocalyptic horseman described in Revelation proves to be suitable because the story takes places during the influenza pandemic of 1918, which is the biggest public health catastrophe in modern history. ②

Lisa Roney, in "Katherine Anne Porter's *Ship of Fools*: An Interrogation of Eugenics", presents a literary criticism of Katherine Anne Porter's novel *Ship of Fools*, and its exploration of themes of health, morality, and eugenics. Details are given to outline Porter's personal history in relation to the creation of the work, citing her generational exposure to movements of proto-fascism in the 1930s and her own battle with tuberculosis. The novel's expositions of the era's emerging views of health are discussed in-depth. ③

Janis Stout, in "Daughter of a War Lost, Won, and Evaded", discusses the work of American journalist Katherine Anne Porter, centering on her childhood, her family, an unstable mixture of Texas and the South U.S. in her work, and connection of her ideas with the Civil War. It informs that both author Willa Cather and Porter have written on the war and its heritage. ④

---

① Iuchi K. "Katherine Anne Porter's Faithful and Relentless Vision of Death in *Pale Horse, Pale Rider*". The Southern Quarterly, 2015, 53(1): 153-170.

② Davis D A. "The Forgotten Apocalypse: Katherine Anne Porter's *Pale Horse, Pale Rider*, Traumatic Memory, and the Influenza Pandemic of 1918". The Southern Literary Journal, 2011, 43(2): 55-74.

③ Roney L. "Katherine Anne Porter's *Ship of Fools*: An Interrogation of Eugenics". Papers on Language and Literature, 2009, 45(1): 82-107.

④ Stout J. "Daughter of a War Lost, Won, and Evaded". Cather Studies, 2015(10): 133-149.

3. Psychoanalytical Study

Mary E. Titus, in "The 'Booby Trap' of Love: Artist and Sadist in Katherine Anne Porter's Mexico Fiction", discusses writer Katherine Anne Porter's exploration in her works of the issues of power underlying the tradition of romantic love. Topics discussed include interactions between the sexes that are presented as sexualized struggles of dominance and submission, and sadistic goals shared by the male characters. [1]

Lorraine DiCicco, in "The Dis-ease of Katherine Anne Porter's Greensick Girls in *Old Mortality*", discusses the anxiety about coming of age experienced by the three generations of adolescent girl characters in the book *Old Mortality*, by Katherine Anne Porter. Topics discussed include girlhood ambivalence in the context of chlorosis or greensickness; cultural conditions that led to this illness; and power of cultural ideology in shaping and distorting a girl's identity. [2]

4. Gender Study

Anne Goodwyn Jones, in "Gender and the Great War: The Case of Faulkner and Porter", explains the differences in the literary attitudes to gender and to war evident in the works about World War I by William Faulkner and Katherine Anne Porter. Females' typical combat experience such as enforced passivity, entrapment within

---

[1] Titus M E. "The 'Booby Trap' of Love: Artist and Sadist in Katherine Anne Porter's Mexico Fiction". Journal of Modern Literature, 1990, 16(4): 617-634.

[2] DiCicco L. "The Dis-ease of Katherine Anne Porter's Greensick Girls in *Old Mortality*". The Southern Literary Journal, 2001, 33(2): 80-98.

enclosed space, marginalization and a rejection of hierarchy are replicated by many men.①

5. Narrative Study

Katie Owens-Murphy, in "Modernism and the Persistence of Romance", argues that the modernist period is often associated with demystification, disenchantment and disillusionment. While it seems unlikely that many writers in this period would make use of romance, a literary mode that explicitly relies on the magical and fantastical romance remained attractive to a number of modernist writers. Willa Cather's *My Mortal Enemy* and Katherine Anne Porter's *Old Mortality* point to an impulse in modernist narrative that revises romance conventions by blending them with the quotidian. Both texts oscillate between enchantment and realism, advocating romance even as they resist its traditionally harmonious ending by closing on notes of dissonance and uncertainty. These novellas demonstrate modernism's ambivalent relationship to romance in their near-simultaneous disavowal and affirmation of this literary mode, which—however much it is discredited by modernity—manages to retain its force.②

6. Traumatic Study

Laurel Bollinger, in "Trauma, Influenza, and Revelation in Katherine Anne Porter's *Pale Horse, Pale Rider*", presents a criticism on the book *Pale Horse, Pale*

---

① Jones A G. "Gender and the Great War: The Case of Faulkner and Porter". Women's Studies, 1986, 13(1/2): 135-148.
② Owens-Murphy K. "Modernism and the Persistence of Romance". Journal of Modern Literature, 2011, 34(4): 48-62.

Rider, by the American author Katherine Anne Porter. Particular focus is given to how the story reflects the influenza epidemic of 1918. Several other literary depictions of the influenza epidemic in literature are also discussed, including the book *The Autobiography of Alice B. Toklas*, by Gertrude Stein and the book *One of Ours*, by Willa Cather. Details relating to the book's plot and what inspired it are also noted. [①]

7. Post-colonial Study

Chandra Wells, in "'Unable to Imagine Getting on without Each Other': Porter's Fictions of Interracial Female Friendship", examines female friendship within the stories of Katherine Anne Porter's *The Old Order*, a collection of seven short stories. These friendships offer a starting point to delve into interracial and intergenerational relationships between women in the American South. According to the author, these relationships form the core of Porter's revisionism. [②]

8. Biological Study

Darwin Payne, in "Literary Connections: Mark Twain, Katherine Anne Porter, William A. Owens, and Tennessee Williams", profiles some of the greatest literary authors in Texas. This essay talks about Mark Twain, who was considered as America's greatest author, and was connected to Dallas through his "Platonic Sweetheart" Laura Wright. Attention is also given to Katherine Anne Porter, who was

---

① Bollinger L. "Trauma, Influenza, and Revelation in Katherine Anne Porter's *Pale Horse, Pale Rider*". Papers on Language and Literature, 2013, 49(4): 364-389.

② Wells C. "'Unable to Imagine Getting on without Each Other': Porter's Fictions of Interracial Female Friendship". Mississippi Quarterly, 2005, 58(3/4): 761-783.

one of the best female authors, and wrote *Pale Horse*, *Pale Rider*, and *Ship of Fools*. William A. Owens and Tennessee Williams are also mentioned. ①

Thomas F. Walsh, in "The Making of *Flowering Judas*", discusses the autobiographical details in Katherine Anne Porter's story *Flowering Judas*. Topics discussed include comments of Porter on the story; parallel between Porter's life in Mexico and in the story; juxtaposition of violence and death in the story; political dimension in the story; and portrait of Porter's friend Mary Louis Doherty in the story. ②

9. Cultural Study

David Yost, in "The Harm of 'Swedening': Anxieties of Nativism in Katherine Anne Porter's *Noon Wine*", discusses the themes of nationalism and nativism in Katherine Anne Porter's novel *Noon Wine*. It mentions that the novel forms a powerful critique of the conflation of national and racial identities by demonstrating both the hypocrisies of nativist reasoning as well as the violence that it inexorably creates. It cites M. Wynn Thomas, who builds his insightful analysis of the novella around the repeated use of the word stranger, and sees the discussion of foreignness as a theological metaphor for alienation and estrangement, rather than as a commentary on the politics of race and immigration. Also, it cites Darlene Harbour Unrue, who sees the labels of stranger and foreigner as symbolizing the isolation inherent in human nature, rather than in a specific political context. ③

---

① Payne D. "Literary Connections: Mark Twain, Katherine Anne Porter, William A. Owens, and Tennessee Williams". Legacies, 2007, 19(1): 40-51.

② Walsh T F. "The Making of *Flowering Judas*". Journal of Modern Literature, 1985, 12(1): 109-130.

③ Yost D. "The Harm of 'Swedening': Anxieties of Nativism in Katherine Anne Porter's *Noon Wine*". The Southern Literary Journal, 2011, 43(2): 75-86.

Thomas Walsh, in "'That Deadly Female Accuracy of Vision': Katherine Anne Porter and *El Heraldo de Mexico*", reports on writer Katherine Anne Porter's literary meanderings as a visitor to Mexico in the 1920s. Topics discussed include *El Heraldo de Mexico*'s report of Porter's arrival from New York to study and gather material for a book; collaboration with Mexican artist Adolfo Best Maugard in production of Aztec-Mexican pantomimes; and literary reviews that Porter wrote for *El Heraldo de Mexico*.[1]

10. Feminism Study

Ellen Matlok-Ziemann, in "Southern Fairy Tales: Katherine Anne Porter's *The Princess* and Carson McCullers's *The Ballad of the Sad Café*", presents a comparison of the literary styles of women writers Katherine Anne Porter and Carson McCullers in fairy tales with special reference to Porter's *The Princess* and McCullers's *The Ballad of the Sad Café*. Porter and McCullers are stated to have subverted the traditional form of the fairy tale by creating strong and independent female protagonists not constrained by gender norms of patriarchal society in the above-mentioned tales.[2]

Andrea K. Frankwitz, in "Katherine Anne Porter's Miranda Stories: A Commentary on the Cultural Ideologies of Gender Identity", discusses the treatment of women in the short stories of Katherine Anne Porter. Topics discussed include an examination of the recurring character of Miranda; a depiction of a passive acceptance of the patriarchal order; the characterization of rebellion against a patriarchal system;

---

[1] Walsh T. "'That Deadly Female Accuracy of Vision': Katherine Anne Porter and *El Heraldo de Mexico*". Journal of Modern Literature, 1990, 16(4): 635-643.

[2] Matlok-Ziemann E. "Southern Fairy Tales: Katherine Anne Porter's *The Princess* and Carson McCullers's *The Ballad of the Sad Café*". Mississippi Quarterly, 2007, 60(2): 257-272.

and implication of the illusory nature of a genderless reality. [1]

Juanita Cabello, in "On the Touristic Stage of 1920s and '30s Mexico: Katherine Anne Porter and a Modernist Tradition of Women Travel Writers", focuses on the short stories *Flowering Judas*, *The Fig Tree*, and *Hacienda* by Katherine Anne Porter. According to the author, Porter's depictions of Mexico drew on traditions from U.S. touristic travel writing about the country and from modernist women's travel writing. Particular focus is given to gender politics in Mexico. It is suggested that while Mexico was often thought to be a site of mobility or escape for women, Porter's travel writing proved otherwise. [2]

11. Comparative Study

Janis P. Stout, in "'The Nude Had Descended the Staircase': Katherine Anne Porter Looks at Willa Cather Looking at Modern Art", points out that both Katherine Anne Porter and Willa Cather are great authors. The author of this essay notes that Porter has made essay for Cather entitled "Reflections on Willa Cather", in which its allusion is a painting entitled "Nude Descending a Staircase (No. 2)", by Marcel Duchamp. The author of this essay cites that Porter has assumed that the readers will understand what is the significance of the Cather's allusion. The author also argues that the essay *Reflections on Willa Cather* is a duplicitous essay in which Porter is considered as an icon of literary modernism. [3]

---

[1] Frankwitz A K. "Katherine Anne Porter's Miranda Stories: A Commentary on the Cultural Ideologies of Gender Identity". Mississippi Quarterly, 2004, 57(3): 473-488.

[2] Cabello J. "On the Touristic Stage of 1920s and '30s Mexico: Katherine Anne Porter and a Modernist Tradition of Women Travel Writers". Women's Studies, 2012, 41(4): 413-435.

[3] Stout J P. "'The Nude Had Descended the Staircase': Katherine Anne Porter Looks at Willa Cather Looking at Modern Art". Cather Studies, 2011(9): 225-243.

Chapter 16

Richard Wright

Richard Wright(1908-1960)

Richard Wright's career can be described in terms of three reputations he has earned: the realist protesting racial oppression, the typifier of the experience of entry into modern history, and the author who makes his themes seen inevitable of his artistry. In the best recent criticism, these three reputations coalesce, and the different levels of significance in his writing are explored. Wright was aware of his race and his dissent from the culture of his native land, first as radical, then as expatriate.

Critical Perspectives

1. Thematic Study

Julia Istomina, in "The Terror of Ahistoricity: Reading the Frame(-up) through and against Film Noir in Richard Wright's *The Man Who Lived Underground*", argues that Richard Wright's *The Man Who Lived Underground* resists narrative cohesion to a greater extent than do the majority of Wright's other literary works. This paper proposes that applying the formal and critical techniques of film noir as a frame through which to process the novella facilitates a deeper analysis of Wright's methods for illustrating the mechanisms of modern racialization. Reading the work through and against the framing devices of film noir also allows for an exploration of the author's ways of theorizing (in) visibility and dispossession that trouble some of the universalizing tendencies of early film noir and humanist philosophical perspectives more broadly. The novella's depiction of the police's framing of an innocent African American watchman for the murder of a white woman is discussed. [1]

2. New-historicism

Melissa Ryan, in "Dangerous Refuge: Richard Wright and the Swimming

---

[1] Istomina J. "The Terror of Ahistoricity: Reading the Frame(-up) through and against Film Noir in Richard Wright's *The Man Who Lived Underground*". African American Review, 2016, 49(2): 111-127.

Hole", looks at Richard Wright's *Big Boy Leaves Home* as a story about swimming—that is, about a natural world claimed as white property and marked "No Trespassing"—finding in Wright's swimming hole an oblique echo of other bodies of water segregated by violence, from Lake Michigan to municipal pools. ①

John Zheng, in "The Many Influences of Richard Wright: An Interview with Jerry W. Ward, Jr.", presents an interview with Jerry W. Ward, Jr., professor of English and African World Studies at Dillard University in New Orleans, Louisiana. When asked about researching author Richard Wright, he mentions reading the book *Uncle Tom's Children* and his background in literary theory and criticism. When asked about the difference between the books *Black Boy* and *American Hunger*, he talks about life during the Jim Crow era. Other topics include alienation and interdisciplinary research. ②

Jerry W. Ward, Jr., in "Blueprints for Engagement: A Retrospective on the 2008 Richard Wright Centennial", presents a literary criticism of the novels *The Long Dream* and *A Father's Law* by Richard Wright, as well as an examination of the conferences and other events held to commemorate the centennial of Wright's birth in 2008. Brief summaries of events related to the centennial in the U.S. and other countries are presented. The extensive nature of the centennial is linked to literary criticism on Wright published by other critics in 2008-2009. The author then considers the two novels in terms of how Wright treats the relationship between fathers and sons and his depiction of African American middle class life. ③

Tara T. Green, in "Meeting Richard Wright in the Mountains: Reflections on

---

① Ryan M. "Dangerous Refuge: Richard Wright and the Swimming Hole". African American Review, 2017, 50(1): 27-40.

② Zheng J. "The Many Influences of Richard Wright: An Interview with Jerry W. Ward, Jr.". African American Review, 2017, 50(1): 17-25.

③ Ward J W Jr. "Blueprints for Engagement: A Retrospective on the 2008 Richard Wright Centennial". The Southern Quarterly, 2010, 47(2): 101-121.

Teaching at Northern Arizona University", discusses the author's experiences teaching the literature of 20th-century African American author Richard Wright at Northern Arizona University, where blacks are a small minority of the student population. This essay discusses introducing the history of lynchings and racial violence in the U.S. through Wright's works to students. ①

Candice Love Jackson, in "Tougaloo College, Richard Wright, and Me: Teaching Wright to the Millennial Student", describes the author's experiences teaching an English course on the 20th-century African American author Richard Wright at Tougaloo College in Mississippi. The reactions of 21st-century students at the historically black college to the perspectives on race and other social issues in Wright's fiction are discussed. ②

Nancy Dixon, in "Did Richard Wright Get It Wrong?: A Spanish Look at *Pagan Spain*", explores possible misconceptions of Richard Wright concerning Spain and considers the reasons for Spanish aversion to the book *Pagan Spain*. The book has largely been ignored by Spaniards due to Wright's subjectivity and interpretation towards Spanish history. Critics infer that Wright lacked the insider status and Spanish language skills that were needed to give the book more depth, while some American readers would argue that Wright did not have the right to judge the decadence of a Christian country since he did not believe in religion. According to the author, *Pagan Spain* is more critical of oppressed Spaniards than of the oppressive regime during the 1950s. ③

---

① Green T T. "Meeting Richard Wright in the Mountains: Reflections on Teaching at Northern Arizona University". Papers on Language and Literature, 2008, 44(4): 382-387.
② Jackson C L. "Tougaloo College, Richard Wright, and Me: Teaching Wright to the Millennial Student". Papers on Language and Literature, 2008, 44(4): 374-381.
③ Dixon N. "Did Richard Wright Get It Wrong?: A Spanish Look at *Pagan Spain*". Mississippi Quarterly, 2008, 61(4): 581-591.

3. Psychoanalytical Study

Jay-Paul Hinds, in "Redemptive Prose: Richard Wright's Re-authoring of the Patricidal Urtext", argues that the adage "the pen is mightier than the sword", written by English playwright Edward Bulwer-Lytton, is a concise declaration that calls attention to the potency of the written word. By no means the exclusive preserve of the political revolutionary (e. g., Marx and Engel's *Manifesto of the Communist Party*) nor of the theological reformer (e. g., Luther's *The Ninety-Five Theses*), the mighty pen is also an instrument used by persons who seek either to effect or to experience a change in a number of diverse, and sometimes more personal, issues. As readers, we often ignore that many authors may be working through their own turmoil—whether psychological, spiritual, or otherwise—when they clasp the pen to put their thoughts to paper. How, then, do authors use the pen as a therapeutic tool to remedy their inner wounds, the unseen trauma often caused by various "psychosocial swords"? This article offers a particularized response to this inquiry by investigating the pain of paternal abandonment and the restorative efficacy of filial wisdom evinced in Richard Wright's novels *Black Boy* and *The Long Dream*. It is the author's contention that Wright's redemptive prose presents convincing evidence that the pen, as an instrument of restoration, is indeed mightier than any sword used to sever those inalienable relationships (e. g., the father-son dyad) that give sustenance to and are therefore an essential part of one's selfhood.[①]

Chen Xu, in "On 'Third Consciousness' in the Fiction of Richard Wright", discusses the triple awareness among African Americans and how that is represented in the fiction of Richard Wright. The idea of double awareness was written about by

---

[①] Hinds J-P. "Redemptive Prose: Richard Wright's Re-authoring of the Patricidal Urtext". Pastoral Psychology, 2013, 62(5): 687-707.

historian W. E. B. Du Bois in *The Souls of Black Folk*, and a comparison is drawn between this idea and Wright's triple awareness. Triple-consciousness is comprised of African American culture, Caucasian culture, and the desire by African Americans to thrive in Caucasian culture.①

Laura Dubek, in "'Til Death Do Us Part: White Male Rage in Richard Wright's *Savage Holiday*", discusses the depiction of the psychotic and oppressive white male in Richard Wright's novel, *Savage Holiday*. *Savage Holiday* emphasizes Wright's commitment to critique American culture, and his fascination with Freudian psychology. Critics aver that the novel invites readers to sympathize with the Oedipal complex that has afflicted the main character. The article presents the symbolism and contradictions attached to the novel's characters and their linkage to historical figures and events. In relation to this, *Savage Holiday* is said to reveal the process for rationalizing the rage of the white male and suggests the dangers that domesticity can impose on white women.②

Dorothy Stringer, in "Psychology and Black Liberation in Richard Wright's *Black Power* (1954)", discusses Wright's travel narrative of the Gold Coast/Ghana, and particularly the politicized psychology it develops as an analytic tool. Paying close attention to the effects of colonial economic control on daily life, Wright discusses such classically psychoanalytic concepts as the return of the repressed, the Oedipal conflict, and anal eroticism in terms of West African daily life, often considerably revising both Freudian concepts and his own notion of black identity in the process. While the African American tradition gave him the means to articulate psychic life with historical realities, the Freudian intervention gave him license to focus on sexual and scatological topics that had yet, in 1954, to receive serious consideration as

---

① Chen Xu. "On 'Third Consciousness' in the Fiction of Richard Wright". The Black Scholar, 2009, 39(1/2): 40-45.
② Dubek L. "'Til Death Do Us Part: White Male Rage in Richard Wright's *Savage Holiday*". Mississippi Quarterly, 2008, 61(4): 593-613.

political matters. Hence, *Black Power* is an enormous resource for contemporary critical efforts towards reading psychoanalysis, African American culture, and political struggles of the global South in combination. ①

4. Marxism Study

Juan D. Gómez, in "Socialism and Identity in the Life and Works of Richard Wright", argues that Richard Wright was a pioneer in American Literature, whose relationship with socialism helped to define him as a person and as a writer. The inspiration behind his literary accomplishments and their impact on his contemporaries can be understood by tracing two of the most important themes in his life: socialism and identity. This article describes the evolution of his relationship with socialism in order to better understand the writer and his best known works in their social and political context. This exercise can also help us to gain a clearer understanding of the cultural and social implications of socialist ideology in the United States after the World War I. ②

Alexa Weik, in "'The Uses and Hazards of Expatriation': Richard Wright's Cosmopolitanism in Process", presents an analysis regarding Richard Wright's outlook of cynic cosmopolitanism. It examines his life and works and the development of his outlook starting from a specific geo-historical position which continue to strive for human solidarity across national and racial boundaries. It states that his marginalized position within the U.S. society had led him to ask questions of race and nation. It concludes that his life demonstrates the difficulty of transcending one's

---

① Stringer D. "Psychology and Black Liberation in Richard Wright's *Black Power* (1954)". Journal of Modern Literature, 2009, 32(4): 105-124.

② Gómez J D. "Socialism and Identity in the Life and Works of Richard Wright". La Palabra, 2015 (27): 33-43.

historical situatedness and the set of prejudices that come along with it.①

Vincent Pérez, in "Movies, Marxism, and Jim Crow: Richard Wright's Cultural Criticism", discusses cultural and media criticism in novelist Richard Wright's works. Topics discussed include Wright's engagement with media culture; two lines of cultural inquiry; twofold nature of Wright's own cultural project; and Wright's three books which highlights cultural conjunctures.②

5. Post-colonial Study

Gregory Phipps, in "'He Wished That He Could Be an Idea in Their Minds': Legal Pragmatism and the Construction of White Subjectivity in Richard Wright's *Native Son*", critiques Richard Wright's *Native Son*, which addresses issues central to African American identity and the identity of the American people at large. Topics discussed include the author's argument that there is a reciprocal interplay between the growth of the character Bigger Thomas' self-consciousness and the collective psyche and the social anxiety about whiteness during the interwar period due to the increasingly diverse array of ethnicities.③

Benjamin Anastas, in "Teaching the Controversy", presents literary criticism of several books by James Baldwin and Richard Wright, including Wright's *Native Son* and Baldwin's *Go Tell It on the Mountain* and *The Fire Next Time*. Particular focus is given to the author's experience of teaching a class on Baldwin and Wright at

---

① Weik A. "'The Uses and Hazards of Expatriation': Richard Wright's Cosmopolitanism in Process". African American Review, 2007, 41(3): 459-475.
② Pérez V. "Movies, Marxism, and Jim Crow: Richard Wright's Cultural Criticism". Texas Studies in Literature and Language, 2001, 43(2): 142-168.
③ Phipps G. "'He Wished That He Could Be an Idea in Their Minds': Legal Pragmatism and the Construction of White Subjectivity in Richard Wright's *Native Son*". Texas Studies in Literature and Language, 2015, 57(3): 325-342.

Bennington College in 2014 and 2015. Details on the social and political context of the class, including racial tensions surrounding the police killings of several young Black men, are presented. ①

Dwayne Marshall Baker, in "Eradicating Blackness: Violence and Humanity in the Works of Richard Wright", argues that the purpose of this essay is to highlight the ability to take control of one's own environment and to determine one's own existence as expressed by Richard Wright. In attempting to fulfill this objective, this essay seeks to challenge notions of individual as well as group identity, especially among blacks within the United States. Primarily, it attempts to answer how blacks identify themselves, whether through immediate and collective needs or based upon pre-determined or pre-destined ideologies. Wright, as the author, sees no good in the continued embracing of race—as it stems from pre-determined ideologies. Therefore, its main argument is that Wright views blackness and black culture as negative determinants of human existence. Richard Wright's *The Outsider* is the primary work addressed as it most aptly addresses the need to re-create one's self. Here, Wright highlights the complete (r)evolution of the main character, Cross Damon, as he struggles to live out his own humanity. Similarly, Wright's *The Long Dream* is analyzed to indicate the inhumanity Wright perceives in the concept of race. In conjunction, the two works show how inhumane the concept of race is, and he seeks to eradicate it, replacing it with a new form of human relationships. ②

Julian Kunnie, in "Richard Wright's Interrogation of Negritude: Revolutionary Implications for Pan Africanism and Liberation", discusses the critical insights of African-American author and critic Richard Wright of negritude in the wake of Western European colonial hegemony. It explores his advocacy of solidarity for all

---

① Anastas B. "Teaching the Controversy". The New Republic, 2015, 246(5): 56-59.
② Baker D M. "Eradicating Blackness: Violence and Humanity in the Works of Richard Wright". The Researcher: An Interdisciplinary Journal, 2012, 25(2): 9-25.

colonized and colored people of the world and the revolutionary implications of his work for Pan-Africanism and liberation. It mentions his involvement in *Présence Africaine* magazine which addresses the themes of colonization and oppression in Africa and the Diaspora. [1]

Sostene Massimo Zangari, in "Straightjacketed into the Future: Richard Wright and the Ambiguities of Decolonization", focuses on Richard Wright's books *Black Power*, written about the Gold Coast, and *The Color Curtain*, written about Indonesia. Wright wrote the books after visiting the two countries in the 1950s, at a time when both nations were dealing with issues of decolonization. He visited the Gold Coast in 1953 by invitation of the country's Prime Minister Kwame Nkrumah. He attended the Bandung Conference of 1955 in Bandung, Indonesia as an independent observer. Wright's observations about problems faced by developing countries, post-colonialism, and communism are discussed. [2]

Katherine Henninger, in "Zora Neale Hurston, Richard Wright, and the Postcolonial Gaze", examines the photographic activities of sociological and anthropological investigators, Richard Wright and Zora Neale Hurston in the Southern States. Topics discussed include rethinking of postcolonial theories of the photographic gaze; readings of images in a relation or exchange; and identitarian lines between the colonized and the colonizers. [3]

6. Biological Study

Howard Rambsy, in "Re-presenting *Black Boy*: The Evolving Packaging History

---

[1] Kunnie J. "Richard Wright's Interrogation of Negritude: Revolutionary Implications for Pan Africanism and Liberation". Journal of Pan African Studies, 2012, 4(9): 1-23.

[2] Zangari S M. "Straightjacketed into the Future: Richard Wright and the Ambiguities of Decolonization". The Black Scholar, 2009, 39(1/2): 78-83.

[3] Henninger K. "Zora Neale Hurston, Richard Wright, and the Postcolonial Gaze". Mississippi Quarterly, 2003, 56(4): 581-596.

of Richard Wright's Autobiography", discusses the changing cover art across various editions of the autobiography *Black Boy* by African American author Richard Wright, from its first publication in 1945 through the 2000s. The covers are considered as different marketing approaches to presenting the book to different generations and several cover images are reproduced and examined. The author discusses how the changing covers provide insight on linguistic and visual elements that connect the different versions of the book. ①

Margaret D. Bauer, in "'Call Me Paul': The Long, Hot Summer of Paul Green and Richard Wright", examines the association between playwright Paul Green and author Richard Wright. It notes several recollections of Green as being more patronizing towards Wright. Green is cited as expressing deep concern that he could have been more understanding towards Wright or developed a closer friendship with him. The article explores the significance of Wright's interview with Green and his appreciation of the playwright's thoughtful treatment of African American issues. It also relates insights regarding aspects of Wright's collaboration with Green including the need to pack a scene with action and making the dialogue and imagery more urban and African-American. ②

7. Philosophical Study

Matthew Briones, in "Call-and-Response: Tracing the Ideological Shifts of Richard Wright through His Correspondence with Friends and Fellow Literati", focuses on African American intellectual and writer Richard Wright. In one concise

---

① Rambsy H. "Re-presenting *Black Boy*: The Evolving Packaging History of Richard Wright's Autobiography". The Southern Quarterly, 2009, 46(2): 71-83.

② Bauer M D. "'Call Me Paul': The Long, Hot Summer of Paul Green and Richard Wright". Mississippi Quarterly, 2008, 61(4): 517-538.

excerpt, Wright emotionally and critically raises a fistful of the major themes of his lifetime's writing: existentialism, the Southern migration and Northern urbanization of mid-century blacks, the hope and failure of Communism, class struggle, black men and white women, and the force of writing itself. The documents chart Wright's consistent disillusionment with the Communist Party and his ongoing quest to write or to aid in writing the great American novel. [①]

8. Cultural Study

Jeff Karem, in "'The Deeper South?': Richard Wright and His Conflicted Views on the Caribbean", discusses the conflicted views of American author Richard Wright on Caribbean culture and practices. Also cited are Wright's works like his autobiography *American Hunger* and the poetic-ethnographic study *12 Million Black Voices*, as well as Wright's views on racial politics and his unpublished Haitian travel writing articles called "Haitian Biographies". [②]

William Ferris, in "Richard Wright and the Blues", explores the relationship of author Richard Wright to the blues culture of African Americans. The blues have captured the imagination of African American writers like Langston Hughes, Ralph Ellison, and Wright. In relation to this, blues music was used as a literary and aesthetic resource for exposing fundamental truths about the experience of African Americans in a predominantly white America. Wright deviated from other African American writers by subscribing to the notion that family, religion, and politics were a

---

① Briones M. "Call-and-Response: Tracing the Ideological Shifts of Richard Wright through His Correspondence with Friends and Fellow Literati". African American Review, 2003, 37(1): 53-64.

② Karem J. "'The Deeper South?': Richard Wright and His Conflicted Views on the Caribbean". The Southern Quarterly, 2018, 55(4): 112-129.

threat to his art and life. The article analyzes parallels between the lives and careers of Wright and fellow writer, Eudora Welty.[1]

9. Spatial Study

Eve Dunbar, in "Black Is a Region: Segregation and American Literary Regionalism in Richard Wright's *The Color Curtain*", offers a literary criticism of *The Color Curtain*, a work by the author Richard Wright. It is reported that this book depicts Wright's struggle with American literary regionalism as a kind of literary segregation. He is said to be attempting to understand black Americans in a global context, while addressing racial segregation in the U.S.[2]

---

[1] Ferris W. "Richard Wright and the Blues". Mississippi Quarterly, 2008, 61(4): 539-552.

[2] Dunbar E. "Black Is a Region: Segregation and American Literary Regionalism in Richard Wright's *The Color Curtain*". African American Review, 2008, 42(1): 109-119.

Chapter 17

Joseph Heller

Joseph Heller (1923-1999)

Joseph Heller is not only regarded as a major contemporary novelist, but also as one who has achieved the rare distinction of balancing academic plaudits with widespread popular success. Even more impressive, the title of his first novel, *Catch-22*, has become a household phrase, one defined by *Wester's New World Dictionary of the American Language* as a paradox in law, regulation, or practice that makes one a victim of its provisions no matter what one does. Heller is widely regarded as one of the best satirists. Although he is remembered mostly by his landmark *Catch-22*, his works, centered on the lives of various members of the middle-classes, remain exceptional exemplars of modern satire.

Critical Perspectives

1. New-historicism

Leah Garrett, in "Joseph Heller's Jewish War Novel *Catch-22*", argues that Joseph Heller's *Catch-22* (1961) is considered as one of the most important American novels of the twentieth century. It was a massive bestseller that sold over 10 million copies, and it introduced a new phrase into the English language for an unsolvable conundrum or paradox. *Catch-22* was groundbreaking because it was the first broadly successful American novel that offered a post-modern and satirical take on the World War II. Ostensibly the novel had nothing whatsoever Jewish about it beyond the ethnicity of its author. Instead it was about the Assyrian/Armenian protagonist, Yossarian, a USAAF bombardier in the European theatre. As the author of this essay argues, while outwardly the novel aims to represent the war and the protagonist, Yossarian, as American rather than Jewish, the work is, in fact, packed with signs that it is about a Jewish airman confronting the Holocaust. Heller's attempt to hide this was part of a tradition established by Jewish authors in the post-war years who sought to distance themselves from their ethnicity in order to speak to "universal" themes of rebellion. However, to overlook the "Jewish" semiotics of *Catch-22* is to miss many of its major themes. This essay thus offers a reading of the novel that will delineate what it tells us about the post-war Jewish life in America. [1]

---

[1] Garrett L. "Joseph Heller's Jewish War Novel *Catch-22*". Journal of Modern Jewish Studies, 2015, 14(3): 391-408.

2. Narrative Study

D. C. Dougherty, in "Nemeses and MacGuffins: Paranoia as Focal Metaphor in Stanley Elkin, Joseph Heller, and Thomas Pynchon", reflects on the use of paranoia as a focal metaphor in novels by Stanley Elkin, Joseph Heller and Thomas Pynchon. Topics discussed include how each author deploys the paranoia metaphor, and motives of the novelists in using the paranoia metaphor. [1]

3. Philosophical Study

Leon F. Seltzer, in "Milo's 'Culpable Innocence': Absurdity as Moral Insanity in *Catch-22*", evaluates the absurdity and moral insanity in Joseph Heller's contemporary novel *Catch-22*. Topics discussed include information on the world of the novel; theme of the book; and main characters of the book. [2]

---

[1] Dougherty D C. "Nemeses and MacGuffins: Paranoia as Focal Metaphor in Stanley Elkin, Joseph Heller, and Thomas Pynchon". Review of Contemporary Fiction, 1995, 15(2): 70-78.

[2] Seltzer L F. "Milo's 'Culpable Innocence': Absurdity as Moral Insanity in *Catch-22*". Papers on Language and Literature, 1979, 15(3): 290-310.

Chapter 18

John Barth

John Barth (1930-)

Highly susceptible to the sport of metaphysical games and passionate attracted to the conundrum of self-consciousness, John Barth has moved steadily away from the objective and realistic toward myth and unashamed fable. His first two novels, *The Floating Opera* and *The End of the Road*, are regarded as twin explorations of the comic and tragic aspects of philosophical nihilism. But his next novel, *The Sot-Weed Factor*, takes an entirely different direction. It is framed on a gigantic scale of multiple plots, disguises, coincidences, intrigues, and deceptions, and it is written in an exuberant and constantly inventive pastiche of 17th-century prose style. History, legend and fiction are mingled in a bawdy, funny, and learned parody of this novel. *The Sot-Weed Factor* purports to chronicle the life and career of Ebenezer Cooke, Poet-Laureate of Maryland. Partly a reinterpretation of the primal fall from innocence, and partly a reexamination of the rich ambiguities in the archetypal American experience, it is both a dazzling tour de force and a major contribution to the novel of fabulation.

Critical Perspectives

1. Gender Study

Agneta Sutton, in "The Complementarity and Symbolism of the Two Sexes: Karl Barth, Hans Urs von Balthasar and John Paul II", compares Hans Urs von Balthasar's, Karl Barth's and Pope John Paul II's views on gender differentiation. It is demonstrated that there is more emphasis on woman's equality with man in the writings of the Pope than in either Barth or Balthasar, even if basically there is no difference between the three theologians in the concept that the creation of man and woman in the image of God is a symbol of the Trinity. [1]

2. Narrative Study

Thomas Carmichael, in "A Postmodern Genealogy: John Barth's *Sabbatical* and *The Narrative of Arthur Gordon Pym*", compares the fiction *Sabbatical*, by John Barth, with the book *The Narrative of Arthur Gordon Pym of Nantucket*, by Edgar Allan Poe. Topics include a discussion on postmodernism; a review of *Sabbatical*; the manipulation of narrative voices in both books; the use of footnotes; and the ambivalence of the literary structure. [2]

---

[1] Sutton A. "The Complementarity and Symbolism of the Two Sexes: Karl Barth, Hans Urs von Balthasar and John Paul II". New Blackfriars, 2006, 87(1010): 418-433.

[2] Carmichael T. "A Postmodern Genealogy: John Barth's *Sabbatical* and *The Narrative of Arthur Gordon Pym*". University of Toronto Quarterly, 1991, 60(3): 389-401.

3. Biological Study

W. Todd Martin, in "Self-Knowledge and Self-Conception: The Therapy of Autobiography in John Barth's *Lost in the Funhouse*", focuses on the novel *Lost in the Funhouse*, by John Barth, which is an autobiography of the character Ambrose. Topics discussed include evaluation of the maze of self-conception; determination of the effects that too much self-knowledge has on the individual; possible ways of dealing with hyper-self-consciousness; and Ambrose's creation of a new identity by rearranging and changing his memory. [1]

4. Philosophical Study

Marc Singer, in "Recursion, Supplementarity, and the Limits of Subjectivity in John Barth's *Menelaiad*", argues that *Menelaiad*, an experimental short story from John Barth's *Lost in the Funhouse*, consists of a series of multiply nested narratives in which each layer recursively generates the next, chronologically earlier one. The story presents narrative and memory as supplemental processes that look back in time to recover or replace a lost moment of presence and completion. Barth suggests these supplements are imperfect and self-defeating means of recapturing the past, however, as they further separate the narrator from his tale's irretrievable origins. The story structures human subjectivity along similarly self-deferring lines, portraying the self not as an essential whole but as a sequence of narrative supplements organized around an absence that no supplement can redress. Paralleling

---

[1] Martin W T. "Self-Knowledge and Self-Conception: The Therapy of Autobiography in John Barth's *Lost in the Funhouse*". Studies in Short Fiction, 1997, 34(2): 151-157.

contemporary developments in poststructuralist theory yet not inspired by, beholden to, or even necessarily aware of them, *Menelaiad* delivers an original illustration of the recursive and supplemental processes that, Barth believes, define and demarcate the human subject. [1]

Christopher Conti, in "Nihilism Negated Narratively: The Agency of Art in *The Sot-Weed Factor*", presents a literary criticism of the book *The Sot-Weed Factor* by John Barth. The author reflects on philosophical aspects of the narrative in relation to themes such as paralysis and mimesis. Other topics include the quest for metaphysical meaning, nihilism, and the novel *The End of the Road*. [2]

---

[1] Singer M. "Recursion, Supplementarity, and the Limits of Subjectivity in John Barth's *Menelaiad*". KronoScope, 2011,10(1): 35-48.

[2] Conti C. "Nihilism Negated Narratively: The Agency of Art in *The Sot-Weed Factor*". Papers on Language and Literature, 2011, 47(2): 141-161.

Chapter 19

Thomas Pynchon

Thomas Pynchon (1937-   )

Thomas Pynchon's novels, *The Crying of Lot 49*, and *Gravity's Rainbow*, have in common qualities that attract some readers and repel others. Both companies of readers are, however, likely to agree on what it is that they respond to in the work of Pynchon. It is an unremitting brilliance of invention, accompanied by a wide range of knowledge. The knowledge embraces the major curse of European history over the past century, and often deviates into nooks and crannies of the entire course of Western experience. In this respect, Pynchon has a novelist's plenty that makes him the peer of John Barth, William Gaddis, and others of his time. The consequence is that one has the sense of reading not only a novel but of progressing through pages from the Britannica, torn out at random.

Critical Perspectives

1. Thematic Study

Vincent King, in "Giving Destruction a Name and a Face: Thomas Pynchon's *Mortality and Mercy in Vienna*", talks about the responsibility of author Thomas Pynchon, his character Cleanth Siegel in the novel *Mortality and Mercy in Vienna* and the reader for their words, taking into account the massacre of unsuspecting victims at a Washington party in the novel. Topics discussed include responsibility of Pynchon; his protagonist in the crime committed by another character; and Pynchon's exploration of the moral cost of reading. [1]

2. New-historicism

Riley McDonald, in "The Frame-Breakers: Thomas Pynchon's Post-human Luddites", argues that Thomas Pynchon's *Vineland* depicts an America moving inexorably toward what Gilles Deleuze calls a "control society", one where intangible power structures enmesh agentless subjects. This article elaborates on the ways radical politics must be met by an equally revolutionary reconceptualization of the body. While, in *Vineland*, the activist film collective 24fps attempts to resist governmental power, their instrumentalization of their media technology (the film

---

[1] King V. "Giving Destruction a Name and a Face: Thomas Pynchon's *Mortality and Mercy in Vienna*". Studies in Short Fiction, 1998, 35(1): 13-21.

camera) leads to their own appropriation by hegemonic forces. Instead, it is the Thanatoids, liminal creatures inextricably linked with the television, who disrupt the control apparatus and present both a resistant (post) human body and a revolutionary new politics. ①

David Cowart, in "Pynchon, Genealogy, History: *Against the Day*", critiques the novel *Against the Day* by Thomas Pynchon, with particular focus given to Pynchon's treatment of history. The concept of a genealogical approach to history in the novel is discussed, and criticism of the genre of historical fiction is examined. Also touched on are the novel's themes of the search for knowledge, modernization, and political power. ②

Ecaterina Pătrașcu, in "Historical Anomie and the Crisis of Identity in Thomas Pynchon's Novels", brings in the limelight preoccupations typical for the postmodern American novel: the anomie of history, the maladive reality, the sterile imagination, and direct consequences of the construction of identity. The approach to these concerns is interdisciplinary, the postmodern concepts of relativism, arbitrary meaning, subjectivity, constructed reality, (his)story and interchangeable interpretations being identified and delineated both in philosophy and literary theory. Perceived from the perspective of quantum physics, historicism in Pynchon is entirely subjective; the organizing structures of history are only products of one's imagination, therefore the anomie and the accidental indubitably govern it. The general impression is that of a paranoid state of mind that evolves from a personal (Herbert Stencil and Oedipa Maas) to a cosmic level (Tyrone Slothrop). ③

---

① McDonald R. "The Frame-Breakers: Thomas Pynchon's Post-human Luddites". Canadian Review of American Studies, 2014, 44(1): 101-121.

② Cowart D. "Pynchon, Genealogy, History: *Against the Day*". Modern Philology, 2012, 109 (3): 385-407.

③ Pătrașcu E. "Historical Anomie and the Crisis of Identity in Thomas Pynchon's Novels". Philobiblon: Transylvanian Journal of Multidisciplinary Research in Humanities, 2011, 16(2): 358-385.

Luc Herman and John M. Krafft, in "Fast Learner: The Typescript of Pynchon's *V.* at the Harry Ransom Center in Austin", discuss the development of the novel *V.* by Thomas Pynchon with the acquisition of its corrected typescript by the Harry Ransom Humanities Research Center at the University of Texas at Austin. It presents that with this acquisition, the reconstruction of materials was made possible and they revealed Pynchon as having mastered the art of novel writing fast. It puts to rest the rumor that Pynchon finished writing *V.* while living in Mexico. ①

William E. Engel, in "Darkness Visible: Pynchon at Seventy", presents a commentary on the literary creation entitled "Against the Day" by Thomas Pynchon. The author comments on Pynchon's publicity and renders perspectives on the creation's plot and theme in which entropy is the main focus. He also comments on Pynchon's notoriety status and his other novels. ②

David Cowart, in "Cinematic Auguries of the Third Reich in *Gravity's Rainbow*", discusses references to German cinema in the novel *Gravity's Rainbow*, by Thomas Pynchon. Topics discussed include the allusions to *Die Frau im Mond*, a movie directed by Fritz Lang; the fascination of the rocket technician character Franz Pokler with Fritz Lang movies; and the picture of Nazi Germany with non-Aryan slave labor at the bottom and a paternal Fuhrer at the top. ③

Elizabeth Jane Wall Hinds, in "Visible Tracks: Historical Method and Thomas Pynchon's *Vineland*", focuses on the use of paranoia as a subject and method of Thomas Pynchon's novels, particularly in *Vineland*. Topics discussed include description of the novel's Prairie Wheeler; Prairie's history making in *Vineland*;

---

① Herman L, Krafft J M. "Fast Learner: The Typescript of Pynchon's *V.* at the Harry Ransom Center in Austin". Texas Studies in Literature and Language, 2007, 49 (1): 1-20.

② Engel W E. "Darkness Visible: Pynchon at Seventy". The Sewanee Review, 2008, 116(4): 660-666.

③ Cowart D. "Cinematic Auguries of the Third Reich in *Gravity's Rainbow*". Literature Film Quarterly, 1978, 6(4): 364-370.

background on Pynchon's Puritan history; pattern of coincidence in the story; and historical method used in the novel. ①

3. Psychoanalytical Study

Debra A. Moddelmog, in "The Oedipus Myth and Reader Response in Pynchon's *The Crying of Lot 49*", examines what role the Oedipus myth plays in Thomas Pynchon's novel *The Crying of Lot 49*. Topics discussed include reason the Oedipus myth functions significantly in the novel, and examples of identifying correspondences between the text and the myth. ②

4. Narrative Study

Aura Sibişan, in "Intertextuality and Thomas Pynchon's Entropy", discusses relevant aspects raised by Linda Hutcheon in her famous book *A Poetics of Postmodernism: History, Theory, Fiction*, and aspects of Thomas Pynchon's work that illustrate intertextuality through the discussion of a scientific concept in a literary work—*Entropy*. The view towards intertextuality has been changed since the 1969 essay of Julia Kristeva. The exploration of scientific visions of the world is a major concern for Thomas Pynchon. Entropy has become an important metaphor of the contemporary world's tendency towards redundancy and incoherence. Pynchon's vision is revealed through his complicated plots, his idealistic characters and a questioning narrative voice. The short story *Entropy* and aspects of the novel *V.* are

---

① Hinds E J W. "Visible Tracks: Historical Method and Thomas Pynchon's *Vineland*". College Literature, 1992,19(1): 91-103.

② Moddelmog D A. "The Oedipus Myth and Reader Response in Pynchon's *The Crying of Lot 49*". Papers on Language and Literature, 1987, 23(2):240-249.

further discussed in the paper. The image of literature as a network of texts was intensified by Derrida's argument about the "impossibility of living outside the text". [1]

David Schell, in "Engaging Foundational Narratives in Morrison's *Paradise* and Pynchon's *Mason & Dixon*", examines how Toni Morrison's *Paradise* and Thomas Pynchon's *Mason & Dixon* construct foundational narratives as critiques of national imaginings. Setting up the idea of the nation as imagined communities coming together through shared narratives, Morrison and Pynchon probe the possibility of future national imaginings through narratives which continually breakdown in establishing the past. In the seeming paradox of narrating pasts that destroy and delimit the future, their novels display the disjuncture between the need to narrate the nation and the collective narratives that often emerge to define national boundaries. Their texts point toward the limits of national imaginings and spaces that unsuccessfully map onto the populations they purport to represent. In the context of the transnational turn in American studies, foundational narratives signal national narratives as self-destructive operations of power that can compel a populace to construct space-less histories and obscure social relations. Simultaneously, foundational narratives can also signal spaces beyond national boundaries, and understandings of the nation as transnational and reliant on fictional modes in order to reestablish historical and social links. [2]

5. Traumatic Study

Arin Keeble, in "*Bleeding Edge*, Neo-Liberalism, and the 9/11 Novel",

---

[1] Sibişan A. "Intertextuality and Thomas Pynchon's Entropy". Bulletin of the Transilvania University of Brasov, Series IV: Philology & Cultural Studies, 2017(2): 103-116.

[2] Schell D. "Engaging Foundational Narratives in Morrison's *Paradise* and Pynchon's *Mason & Dixon*". College Literature, 2014, 41(3): 69-94.

argues that Thomas Pynchon's *Bleeding Edge* (2013) can be read within the canon of 9/11 novels in unexpected and productive ways. Its rich, intertwined narrative of the Internet and 9/11 both echoes early 9/11 novels and departs from them as it builds a trenchant critique of neo-liberalism. [1]

6. Religious Study

Joshua Pederson, in "The Gospel of Thomas (Pynchon): Abandoning Eschatology in *Gravity's Rainbow*", reads Thomas Pynchon's sprawling masterpiece *Gravity's Rainbow*—with its shell-shocked refugees fleeing across a missile-pocked, post-war landscape—as an eschatological text that plays out religious end-times scenarios. However, an invented citation from the non-canonical Gospel of Thomas included as a chapter epigraph—"Dear Mom, I put a couple of people in hell today"—suggests that we should do otherwise. In grafting a playful fragment about Jesus, judgment, and hell onto Thomas, Pynchon parodies a common need to read eschatological themes back into non-eschatological texts. In doing so, he also provides a powerful heuristic for interpreting his own book. Ultimately, Pynchon's own rocket-gospel is likewise a non-eschatological text. Like Thomas, *Gravity's Rainbow* stymies readers' efforts to derive a clear eschatology from it—or to read one back into it. In this essay, the author contends that Pynchon enacts a number of strategies to keep his audience from reading classic end-times scenarios into his own work, all of which are prefigured by the *Gospel of Thomas*. [2]

---

[1] Keeble A. "*Bleeding Edge*, Neo-Liberalism, and the 9/11 Novel". Canadian Review of American Studies, 2019, 49(3): 249-270.

[2] Pederson J. "The Gospel of Thomas (Pynchon): Abandoning Eschatology in *Gravity's Rainbow*". Religion and the Arts, 2010, 14(1): 139-160.

7. Canonization Study

Scott Simmon, in "Beyond the Theater of War: *Gravity's Rainbow* as Film", considers the theater-of-war metaphor in the novel *Gravity's Rainbow*, by Thomas Pynchon. Topics discussed include the desires and fears which threaten to destroy Western Civilization, and explicit and implicit references to Hollywood genre films of the 1930s and 1940s, and German expressionist cinema of the 1920s. [1]

8. Biological Study

Nick Levey, in "Mindless Pleasures: Playlists, Unemployment, and Thomas Pynchon's *Inherent Vice*", argues that Thomas Pynchon's *Inherent Vice* is his least interesting work. But the lack of critical consideration has less to do with the quality of the novel, than with the challenge it puts to readers of contemporary fiction. Throughout *Inherent Vice*, Pynchon attempts to alter how we approach the task of reading maximalist novels in the age of the Internet. Pynchon's citation of his own references, gaming with ontological clarity, and celebration of cloudy intellectual powers, are strategies he employs in *Inherent Vice* to reevaluate what novels can offer us in the twenty-first century. [2]

Michael Hartnett, in "Thomas Pynchon's Long Island Years", provides information on the life and works of Thomas Pynchon in Long Island, New York. The author stated that Pynchon has been born on May 8, 1937 in Glen Cove, Long

---

[1] Simmon S. "Beyond the Theater of War: *Gravity's Rainbow* as Film". Literature/Film Quarterly, 1978, 6(4): 347-363.

[2] Levey N. "Mindless Pleasures: Playlists, Unemployment, and Thomas Pynchon's *Inherent Vice*". Journal of Modern Literature, 2016, 39(3): 41-56.

Island and then move to nearby East Norwich, where he lived until he graduated at Oyster Bay High School as salutatorian at the age of 16. He added that Pynchon has written about misfits like trigonometry teacher Faggiaducci, who seems to endure through a combination of heroin-intake and be-bop talking in November 13, 1952 column. Moreover, Pynchon shows a rudimentary grasp of the psychological responses and societal mechanisms that constitutes a large part of his later writings at the age of 15. [1]

9. Philosophical Study

Abdullah H. Kurraz, in "Analogizing Jean Baudrillard's America and Thomas Pynchon's *The Crying of Lot 49*: Entropy Imagery of the Puzzled", argues that in *The Crying of Lot 49*, Thomas Pynchon presents a postmodern society of a huge replication of puzzling out of symbols and ciphers of entropy, which result in an immense number of interpretations and reflections. Therefore, the authentic interpretative communities of these allusions in Pynchon's narrative are both overwhelmingly definite and entropic. The sole protagonist in *The Crying of Lot 49*, Oedipa, is loaded by a chaotic information overflow that yields anarchy and uncertainty. She also cannot find convincing answers to the mysterious yet realistic questions, hence, she gets alienated in the hyperreal puzzling world of uncorrelated information. Oedipa becomes mentally disoriented and indifferent as a result of the dominant hyperreality in the postmodern world. *The Crying of Lot 49* portrays a modern society full of codified signs and simulation. This study used qualitative

---

[1] Hartnett M. "Thomas Pynchon's Long Island Years". Confrontation, 2008(101): 34-35.

research method to trace and explain various analogies and commonalities between the two authors and their postmodernist texts. [1]

10. Translation Study

Rebecca Schönsee, in "No Light against Entropy: Elfriede Jelinek's Translation of Thomas Pynchon's *Gravity's Rainbow* and Its Impact on *Die Kinder der Toten*", argues that Elfriede Jelinek's unique translation of the title of Thomas Pynchon's *Gravity's Rainbow* (1973) as *Die Enden der Parabel* is representative of the ways in which the Austrian author developed Pynchon's imagery in her work. In shifting focus to the twofold meaning of parable and parabola, her translation becomes an intervention. The article traces Pynchon's impact on Jelinek's writing, in particular on *Die Kinder der Toten*. The article argues that Jelinek engages in a poetic exploration of reclaimed agency in an entropic environment; this is an exploration in which Pynchon's iridescent parables play a pivotal role as agents of self-awareness acting against entropy. [2]

---

[1] Kurraz A H. "Analogizing Jean Baudrillard's America and Thomas Pynchon's *The Crying of Lot 49*: Entropy Imagery of the Puzzled". International Journal of Humanities, Arts & Social Sciences, 2020, 6(6): 234-243.

[2] Schönsee R. "No Light against Entropy: Elfriede Jelinek's Translation of Thomas Pynchon's *Gravity's Rainbow* and Its Impact on *Die Kinder der Toten*". Seminar: A Journal of Germanic Studies, 2021, 57(1): 61-84.

Chapter 20

Donald Barthelme

Donald Barthelme (1931-1989)

Donald Barthelme's literary output is most known for his short stories, with his Postmodern fiction being entirely unique. Indeed, he is considered a pioneer of flash fiction. Barthelme's experimental short stories avoid many of the common traits of a story. Barthelme's short story, *The School*, is an excellent example of his style as a writer. Barthelme is able to take the general concerns of our human condition concerns over the purpose of life or the reasons we die and put them in the mouths of school children. Also, he blends both humor and seriousness in one story.

Critical Perspectives

1. Narrative Study

Nicole Sierra, in "Surrealist Histories of Language, Image, Media: Donald Barthelme's 'Collage Stories'", argues that using previously neglected archival materials from the *Donald Barthelme Literary Papers* at the University of Houston Libraries, this article identifies the sources of Donald Barthelme's collages and their allusive meanings. In doing so, the author's under-appreciated relationship with artistic collage techniques is further elucidated, revealing how indebted his work is to the innovations of surrealist collage production. Principal amongst these influences is Max Ernst's "historical" collage aesthetic. Using the theories of Marshall McLuhan, this article argues that Barthelme's technique of pictorial collage is an attempt to rival contemporary systems of representation (like television and radio), while recognizing the significance of mass media on his work. Capturing the evolving landscape of contemporary mass culture, this article examines the relationship between text and image in Barthelme's short stories. [1]

James McAdams, in "'I Did a Nice Thing': David Foster Wallace and the Gift Economy", offers information on author David Foster Wallace along with his writing styles. Topics discussed include description of his book *The Broom of the System*, a novel with self-indulgent style in 1993; re-evaluation of his approach towards metafictional writing under influence of several writers such as Donald

---

[1] Sierra N. "Surrealist Histories of Language, Image, Media: Donald Barthelme's 'Collage Stories'". European Journal of American Culture, 2013, 32(2): 153-171.

Barthelme; and assessment of Wallace's idiosyncratic characteristic in *Infinite Jest*. [1]

2. Cultural Study

Jaroslav Kušnír, in "Subversion of Myths: High and Low Cultures in Donald Barthelme's *Snow White* and Robert Coover's *Briar Rose*", analyses Donald Barthelme's and Robert Coover's postmodern novels *Snow White* and *Briar Rose* and the way both authors, especially through the use of parody and irony, undermine traditional genres of popular literature and, at the same time, give both an intramural critique of traditional narrative techniques (and the vision of the world they produce) and the extramural critique of consumerism and popular culture. In addition to this, with the analysis of Coover's novel, the emphasis is on the imagery of dreams and dreaming understood as the manifestation of undermining of some aspects of Freudian theories. [2]

---

[1] McAdams J. "'I Did a Nice Thing': David Foster Wallace and the Gift Economy". English Studies in Canada, 2016, 42(3/4):119-133.

[2] Kušnír J. "Subversion of Myths: High and Low Cultures in Donald Barthelme's *Snow White* and Robert Coover's *Briar Rose*". European Journal of American Culture, 2004, 23(1): 31-49.

Chapter 21
Joyce Carol Oates

Joyce Carol Oates (1938-   )

Joyce Carol Oates is an American author born on 16th June 1938 in Lockport, New York. She was very keen on reading and writing from an early age and her first love was a gift from her paternal grandmother—Lewis Carroll's *Alice's Adventures in Wonderland*. Oates considers this book the greatest literary inspiration of her life. Oates graduated in 1956 from Williamsville South High School. She got a scholarship and enrolled in Syracuse University. During this time she read the works of many notable authors such as Flannery O'Connor, Franz Kafka, Henry David Thoreau, Ernest Hemingway and Charlotte Bronte. She graduated as a valedictorian with a degree in English in 1960. She did her Masters from the University of Wisconsin-Madison in 1961.

Her first work was published by Vanguard Press in 1963. It was a short story collection called "By the North Gate". Her first authored novel was called "With Shuddering Fall" and it was published in 1964 followed by *Where Are You Going, Where Have You Been?* in 1966. Her short story titled "In the Region of Ice" was next in 1966 and it won the O. Henry Award. Her 1967 novel was *A Garden of Early Delights*. As a writer, she is highly inspired by Franz Kafka and James Joyce.

Critical Perspectives

1. Psychoanalytical Study

Tatjana Srceva-Pavlovska, in "When Pro-Choice Becomes Anti-Democratic Notion: Pro-Life Lessons on Violence in *A Book of American Martyrs* by J. C. Oates", focuses on the global political aspects of the "pro-life" vs. "prochoice" ideologies, with an accent on the American social, political and religious living vis-a-vis their reflection, implication and repercussions on everyday life, as well as their correlation to a contemporary psychological novel *A Book of American Martyrs* by Joyce Carol Oates. This complex issue is expressed through the acts of severe violence and suffering, manifested through homicide, profound moral erosion, and the deep psychological trauma the entire "pro-life problem" has brought into the lives of many American families. Furthermore, the article analyzes not only the literary analogy of the consequences of this (already) escalated problem as well as its aftermath and its impact on the people's lives, underlying the abandonment, loss, and the dysfunctional relations as a result of it, but also, it further dives into the statistical analysis of the existing problem in real life, in terms of the current abortion numbers and statistics on a broader scale, worldwide and in the United States at present, thus sketching a portrait of multiple perspectives of the violent responses to the imposed restrictions on the freedom of choice, as well as further explaining its medical, philosophical and cultural implications which lead to a current, modern-day general revolt related to the hash obstruction and restriction of the female rights to free and safe abortion. [1]

---

[1] Srceva-Pavlovska T. "When Pro-Choice Becomes Anti-Democratic Notion: Pro-Life Lessons on Violence in *A Book of American Martyrs* by J. C. Oates". Vizione, 2021(37): 369-382.

2. Narrative Study

A. R. Coulthard, in "Joyce Carol Oates's *Where Are You Going, Where Have You Been?* as Pure Realism", discusses the realistic mode used by Joyce Carol Oates in the short story *Where Are You Going, Where Have You Been?*. Topics discussed include Oates' modeling of her story on Charles Schmid's murder of Alleen Rowe in the fall of 1965; Oates' characterization of Arnold Friend; consistent naturalism of the story; and the so-called symbols of Arnold Friend as supernatural demon. [1]

C. Harold Hurley, in "Cracking the Secret Code in Oates's *Where Are You Going, Where Have You Been?*", discusses the biblical interpretation of certain numbers in the short story *Where Are You Going, Where Have You Been?*, by Joyce Carol Oates. Topics discussed include indications of the sexual deviancy of the character Arnold Friend, and ways in which the secret code underscores Arnold's intention of raping and murdering Connie. [2]

3. Biological Study

Elizabeth Lennox Keyser, in "*A Bloodsmoor Romance*: Joyce Carol Oates's *Little Women*", talks about the novel *A Bloodsmoor Romance*, a fictional account by Joyce Carol Oates of the life of Louisa May Alcott, author of *Little Women*. Topics discussed include comments by critics on Alcott's claim that most of the details in

---

[1] Coulthard A R. "Joyce Carol Oates's *Where Are You Going, Where Have You Been?* as Pure Realism". Studies in Short Fiction, 1989, 26(4): 505-510.

[2] Hurley C H. "Cracking the Secret Code in Oates's *Where Are You Going, Where Have You Been?*". Studies in Short Fiction, 1987, 24(1): 62-66.

Little Women is about her and her sisters; basis of Oates' characters; Oates' use of biographies on Alcott as references for her novel; and comparison between characters and events between the two books. ①

4. Feminism Study

Lotta Kähkönen, in "Anxiety about Whiteness in Joyce Carol Oates's Novel *Blonde*", argues that since the beginning of the 1990s, Joyce Carol Oates's fiction manifests increasing interest in the issues of race and ethnicity. Her novel *Blonde* (2000), a fictional depiction of Marilyn Monroe's life, reflects critically the construction of white self, and displays racialization as a complex dialogue between social practices and individual subject constitution. Inspired by critical whiteness studies and feminist theories of intersectionality, this article examines how Oates's novel represents effects of racialization to a white female identity and aims to decipher questions about power and discursive conceptions concerning ideas of race and gender. By giving emphasis to the concepts formation and interface in the US context and American literary tradition, the analysis shows how the construction of the protagonist's gendered and racialized identity is represented as a complex and anxiety-ridden negotiation. The representation of the protagonist's engagement with the white ideal highlights both her desires and anxieties about the idea of race. In so doing, Oates's novel elicits how racialization works both as defining and limiting to white female identity. ②

---

① Keyser E L. "*A Bloodsmoor Romance*: Joyce Carol Oates's *Little Women*". Women's Studies, 1988, 14(3): 211-223.
② Kähkönen L. "Anxiety about Whiteness in Joyce Carol Oates's Novel *Blonde*". NORA: Nordic Journal of Feminist and Gender Research, 2009, 17(4): 289-303.

Susana Isabel Araújo, in "Marriages and Infidelities: Joyce Carol Oates's Way out of the Labyrinths of Metafiction", looks at a crucial period in the shaping of Joyce Carol Oates's short fiction in the early 1970s. This decade witnesses Oates's experiment with a varied range of styles and genres, a move which, in terms of her short fiction, allows a more articulate approach to her various thematic subjects. ①

5. Comparative Study

Nancy Bishop Dessommes, in "O'Connor's Mrs. May and Oates's Connie: An Unlikely Pair of Religious Initiates", compares the women characters of Joyce Carol Oates and Flannery O'Connor. Topics discussed include the characters' self-realization; religious initiation of women characters; problems in characterization; significance of male intruder; expression of anxiety typical of women's dreams; characters' search for identity; characters' fear of the future; and moral and sexual uncertainties. ②

---

① Araújo S I. "Marriages and Infidelities: Joyce Carol Oates's Way out of the Labyrinths of Metafiction". Women's Studies, 2004, 33(1): 103-123.
② Dessommes N B. "O'Connor's Mrs. May and Oates's Connie: An Unlikely Pair of Religious Initiates". Studies in Short Fiction, 1994, 31(3): 433-440.

Chapter 22

Saul Bellow

Saul Bellow (1915-2005)

Since receiving the Nobel Prize in Literature, Saul Bellow has been assured of an important position in American literature, but this position is not really a new one. For more than thirty years, at least since the publication of his popular *The Adventures of Augie March*, Bellow has been heralded as the major spokesman of realism, as the most articulate voice for humanism, as the most sophisticated comedian of the modern predicament, and even as the one on whose shoulders has fallen the mantle of genius previously worn by William Faulkner. No matter how exaggerated these evaluations might seem, Bellow was surely one of the major postwar American novelists.

Critical Perspectives

1. Thematic Study

Jean-François Leroux, in "Exhausting Ennui: Bellow, Dostoevsky, and the Literature of Boredom", reexamines Saul Bellow's much-discussed relationship to Dostoevsky by focusing on the genealogy of boredom, with its dual origins as source of lyrical expression and/or prison of moral ambivalence. Specifically, though Bellow criticism past and present has argued by turns, and sometimes simultaneously, that Bellow is a disciple of Dostoevsky, it finds upon closer inspection that what Bellow truly strives to envisage in/through the glass of Dostoevsky's "Eastern" art is a harmonious resolution to the paradox inherent in this alliance of apparently incompatible ideals—the artist's creed of disinterestedness and the moralist-polemicist's commitment to self-realization through conviction and action. However, where Bellow and his critics see concord, Dostoevsky and his critics see discord. And with reason, Bellow's desire to reconcile the artist and the moralist in Dostoevsky (and in himself) leads him to ignore boredom's moral-intellectual antecedents in the literature of Western Enlightenment and consequently assert his bias as a "spokesman for our culture, a defender of the Western cultural tradition". Conversely, but by the same token, the "constant conflict between the propagandist and creative artist" enacted in Dostoevsky's oeuvre points to his polemic not only with the West but, of course, with himself. [1]

---

[1] Leroux J-F. "Exhausting Ennui: Bellow, Dostoevsky, and the Literature of Boredom". College Literature, 2008, 35(1):1-15.

2. New-historicism

Larissa Sutherland, in "Jewish Poetics in Saul Bellow's *Henderson the Rain King* (1959)", argues that of all the novels in Saul Bellow's oeuvre, *Henderson the Rain King* (1959) seems to be the only one that is unrelated to Jewish life. Its plot revolves around an Anglo-Saxon millionaire, Eugene Henderson, who travels to Africa in search of answers to his existential crisis. This article shows that the novel is actually replete with Jewish themes and it positions the book alongside other postwar texts that disguised Jewish modes of expression within seemingly universal narratives. Henderson is framed in Yiddish and biblical rhetoric and reflects the ideas that Bellow developed in response to the Holocaust. It is also full of contradictions and ambiguities characteristic of this postwar genre; for instance, Henderson is exaggeratedly goyish, at the same time he features many Jewish traits. By bringing attention to these aspects of the novel, this reading engages with critical and theoretical debates around how to demarcate the parameters that define Jewish American literature. It encourages the reader to reconsider those postwar texts that have been misinterpreted as diverging from Jewishness. And it directs them beyond the obvious hallmarks of Jewishness toward subtler cues that account for the ambivalences of postwar Jewish American identification.[①]

Jeet Heer, in "Professor Bellow", discusses the relation of author Saul Bellow to universities in his life and fiction. Topics include his participation in the Committee on Social Thought at the University of Chicago, his novels *Herzog* and *The Dean's December*, and the portrayal of Chicago, Illinois in Bellow's work. His friendship with sociologist Edward Shils is noted. Sexism in the novel *The Dean's*

---

① Sutherland L. "Jewish Poetics in Saul Bellow's *Henderson the Rain King* (1959)". Prooftexts: A Journal of Jewish Literary History, 2018, 37(1): 102-128.

December is addressed. [1]

Rebecca Entel, in "Words that Populate the World: Yiddish and Survival in Saul Bellow's *Herzog*", discusses Saul Bellow's book *Herzog*, which depicts the life of Moses Herzog and his fellow Jews during the time of the holocaust, their assimilation to foreign culture, their life during and after World War II and the use of Yiddish language to communicate with his people. The author also discusses in his letters the execution of the Jews, mass graves and concentration camps during these events. [2]

Faruk Kalay and Bülent C. Tanritanir, in "The Use of History in Nabokov's *Lolita* and Bellow's *Herzog*: Fantasy or Reality?", argue that twentieth-century authors Saul Bellow and Vladimir Nabokov have both made indispensable contributions to American, Jewish, and Russian literature. Bellow's *Herzog* and Nabokov's *Lolita* both feature autobiographical elements, and they draw on history and mythology. However, their historical plots differ from each other on a functional level. Nabokov uses history to realize his fantasies. For instance, Humbert gives examples from the old US' constitutions to sleep with his "nymphet". For Bellow, history is an organ employed to raise society's—especially Jewish society's—historical awareness. The writer who uses examples from historical and philosophical figures makes models. In doing so, he addresses his writing either directly or indirectly toward his readers. Yet these two prominent authors differ significantly from each other in how they take readers to historical places and distinct periods. Their use of history, reality and mythology in their novels is discussed. [3]

---

[1] Heer J. "Professor Bellow". The New Republic, 2015, 246(11): 24-29.

[2] Entel R. "Words that Populate the World: Yiddish and Survival in Saul Bellow's *Herzog*". Australian Journal of Jewish Studies, 2007(21): 27-48.

[3] Kalay F, Tanritanir B C. "The Use of History in Nabokov's *Lolita* and Bellow's *Herzog*: Fantasy or Reality?". Journal of Süleyman Demirel University Institute of Social Sciences, 2014, 19(1): 225-236.

3. Psychoanalytical Study

Robert Chodat, in "Beyond Science and Supermen: Bellow and Mind at Mid-Century", explores Saul Bellow's questioning of how the radically eliminative and idealist dogmas of postmodernism combine in natural superhumanism. Topics discussed include inversion of the expectable postmodernist skepticism about realism; advancement of a chastened form of folk realism to bear on the received ideas of postmodernism; ways in which the work of Bellow could be said to struggle with fundamental elements of the Cartesian legacy; and convergence between Bellow and postpositivist philosophy of mind. [1]

4. Marxism Study

Sukhbir Singh, in "'Socialism of the Soul': Holocaust in Saul Bellow's *The Victim*", argues that Saul Bellow wrote his second novel *The Victim* at the *Partisan Review* group's instance. In the aftermath of the Holocaust, the *Partisan Review* group advocated the assimilation of the American Jews into mainstream American life for their future safety and prosperity. Keeping in view Bellow's creative potentials and belief in Marxism/Trotskyism, the *Partisan Review* members asked him to educate the Jews in this matter through his fiction. Bellow treated the subject of Jewish assimilation in an allegorical vein, projecting the idea of universal brotherhood based on common human grounds. Here, a Jew, Asa Leventhal, behaves like a gentile, and a gentile, Kirby Allbee, behaves like a Jew. They are victims and victimizers of each other. Their repeated encounters mitigate their racial apprehensions and bring the two

---

[1] Chodat R. "Beyond Science and Supermen: Bellow and Mind at Mid-Century". Texas Studies in Literature and Language, 2003, 45(4): 391-425.

closer to each other. Both discover one into the other as his inescapable self, bound by a common human connection. Finally they make peace with each other, projecting Bellow's allegory of inexorable cosmic kinship—"socialism of the soul"—despite their differences of blood, race and religion. [1]

5. Narrative Study

Elonora Hodaj, in "Saul Bellow: Mastery in Handling Humour and Parody", argues that humour in Bellow's prose is both rich and complex, and it helps express the author's propensity for self-analysis and self-scrutinizing heroes. The purpose of this paper is to highlight Bellow's mastery in handling his humour and presenting episodes that are both grotesque and absurd in some of his best novels, such as *Henderson the Rain King*, *Herzog*, *Humboldt's Gift*, *Mr. Sammler's Planet* and *The Dean's December*. The association of the various types of humoristic touches of his novels to the potential effects and functions they play in them remain within the scope of the this paper. [2]

Mark Sandy, in "'Webbed with Golden Lines': Saul Bellow's Romanticism", argues that attaining prominence in the post-war era, Saul Bellow is one of the most widely read and intellectually eclectic novelists of the Jewish American School. Bellow's frequent references to Romanticism form a dominant design within his culturally diverse fiction. Taken from Bellow's *Herzog*, the title of this article indicates the two levels on which Bellow's romantic allusions operate. At one level, this "webbed" pattern of "golden lines" suggests how Bellow interlaces his own prose with the poetry and philosophy of British Romanticism to govern readers' responses to

---

[1] Singh S. "'Socialism of the Soul': Holocaust in Saul Bellow's *The Victim*". Journal of Modern Jewish Studies, 2019, 18(3): 282-297.

[2] Hodaj E. "Saul Bellow: Mastery in Handling Humor and Parody". Bulletin of the Transilvania University of Braşov, Series IV: Philology & Cultural Studies, 2019, 12(2): 155-162.

his portrayal of epiphanies. On another, Herzog's moment of inter-connected vision signals Bellow's investment in a Coleridgean and Wordsworthian imagination. This metaphysical dimension to Bellow's web of "golden lines" finds a further affinity with Shelley's later notion of the "web of being". ①

6. Reader-response Study

Leonard Kriegel, in "Wrestling with Augie March", presents the author's reflections on the novel *The Adventures of Augie March*, by Saul Bellow. The author recalled how this book provided him with his first literary hero in the character Augie, an offspring of Jewish immigrants who succeeds in possessing America by seizing its language for his own. The character lives a compulsively experiential life and is thrown into various adventures by getting into different professions such as training eagles and becoming a merchant marine during a war. ②

7. Post-colonial Study

Eugene Goodheart, in "Kazin, Bellow and Trilling: A Triptych", discusses a short essay by American intellectual and author Alfred Kazin on writers Saul Bellow and Lionel Trilling, which turns into a triptych of all three by illuminating them as writers, Americans and Jews. Topics covered include the reflection of Kazin on Bellow's power of observation and confidence in his destiny as a artist, how Kazin portrays Trilling, and their different attitudes toward America. ③

---

① Sandy M. "'Webbed with Golden Lines': Saul Bellow's Romanticism". Romanticism, 2008, 14(1): 57-67.
② Kriegel L. "Wrestling with Augie March". The Nation, 2003, 276(24): 27-32.
③ Goodheart E. "Kazin, Bellow and Trilling: A Triptych". Society, 2018, 55(6): 503-505.

8. Philosophical Study

John Leonard, in "A Closing of the American Kind", focuses on the novel *Ravelstein*, by Saul Bellow. *Raveistein* is the story of two deaths—of a philosopher and a novelist. In the novel, Abe Ravelstein, a political philosopher just out of intensive care and feeling shaky, is escorted by his friend Chick, a much-married older novelist, from the University of Chicago campus back to his apartment, stopping at every other corner to catch his breath. Thirty pages later, two years after Abe's death, Chick thinks back to "the morning of the day when he had come upon the parrot-filled holly bushes where the birds were feeding on red berries and scattering the snow". Finally, at the end of this lambent novel, this prayer for the dead, Chick seems to be channeling Raveistein. [1]

Bülen Cercis Tanritanir and Özcan Akşak, in "*Henderson the Rain King*: Resolving Existential Despair with Theist Existential Philosophy", point out that Saul Bellow has written in the modern area. Many novelists in this period have seen problems of man that are distinctive and prevalent in the modern period. Philosophical movements in this period have also influenced writers of the time. Existentialism is one of the philosophical movements by which many writers have been influenced. This essay shows Henderson's dissatisfaction with the post-war society in Modern America and Henderson's spiritual transformation in Africa, pointing to the fact that Henderson doesn't reject religion. This essay shows that Bellow uses religious elements in his novel and he approaches Søren Kierkegaard's theist existentialist philosophy, which is based on brotherhood and love. [2]

---

[1] Leonard J. "A Closing of the American Kind". The Nation, 2000, 270(21): 25-30.

[2] Tanritanir B C, Akşak Ö. "*Henderson the Rain King*: Resolving Existential Despair with Theist Existential Philosophy". Atatürk Üniversitesi Sosyal Bilimler Enstitüsü Dergisi, 2010, 14(1): 1-10.